HEARTBREAK AT HAVERSHAM

Beth Carrington is thrilled to be asked to restore the paintings at Haversham Hall, but she soon finds herself enmeshed in the problems of the Tomlin family. Stephen, the elder son of Lord Tomlin, is unhappily married; his brother, Alex, is overbearing and autocratic. When one of Lord Tomlin's paintings disappears, and Stephen's wife, Laura, goes missing, the whole family is surrounded in mystery and Beth is to go through much torment and misery before she finds happiness.

Books by Gillian Kaye
in the Linford Romance Library:

WAITING FOR MATT

GILLIAN KAYE

HEARTBREAK AT HAVERSHAM

Complete and Unabridged

LINFORD
Leicester

First published in Great Britain in 1992 by
Robert Hale Limited
London

First Linford Edition
published 1998
by arrangement with
Robert Hale Limited
London

British Library CIP Data

Kaye, Gillian
    Heartbreak at Haversham.—Large print ed.—
Linford romance library
    1. Love stories
    2. Large type books
    I. Title
    823.9'14 [F]

    ISBN 0–7089–5229–1

Published by
F. A. Thorpe (Publishing) Ltd.
Anstey, Leicestershire

Set by Words & Graphics Ltd.
Anstey, Leicestershire
Printed and bound in Great Britain by
T. J. International Ltd., Padstow, Cornwall

This book is printed on acid-free paper

1

BETH sat at the back of the shop and looked at the calendar that hung by the side of the till. October 31st; always a sad day in the year for her.

Beth was Elizabeth Carrington, and the shop was a small gallery that sold paintings and crafts in the small town of Orborough on the Suffolk coast. And that day, being October 31st signalled for Beth the end of the season and the day she closed the shop for the winter. From Easter and through the summer and autumn, Orborough was a busy town, popular as much for its fine old buildings and the ruins of the castle as for its stretch of coast. No children's paradise, Orborough; the sea, being the North Sea, always cold and the beach composed of pebbles and shingle. The River Orde ran into the sea here and there were many walks along its banks, through the waving reeds and shimmering water of the flat East Anglian landscape.

Beth loved the gallery and the shop that went with it, all aspects of it: the excitement of the hunt for pictures to sell; the contact with the painters and the potters who brought their work to her; and the pleasure of displaying and selling the variety of landscapes and seascapes that came her way. Then there were the people who came to browse and sometimes to buy; visitors were always drawn to the shop and the cheery but not interfering welcome they got from its owner.

For Beth had gone to art college when she left school, and from there on to a two-year course that had trained her to restore paintings; this was the other part of Beth's life. At the back of the shop, she had a studio and there, during the evenings and at weekends, she worked hard at cleaning the pictures that were brought to her and restoring them to their former glory. It was an excitement in itself to see a dark and dirty old painting take on new life and colour once it had been skilfully cleaned.

She had started her training with a firm of restorers in Norwich until she felt she had the experience and the confidence to start up on her own. She had saved hard until she had the chance of buying the Orborough shop. She did not hesitate, she knew she would never make a fortune, but it was what she wanted to do and all her savings went into the purchase of the shop. That had been three years ago, she was now twenty-five and here she was closing at the end of yet another season.

It was her usual custom in the winter to keep herself busy in the studio and to go out hunting for pictures to sell in the next season, but this year she was making enquiries about some pictures that needed restoring in a big house not far from Orborough.

But before she started to think about that, she was going to have a holiday, and then she grinned to herself as she thought of what would happen when she returned. Dave would ask her to marry him.

Dear Dave. He had been the first person she had ever met in Orborough as he was an estate agent and he had shown her the shop and arranged the purchase. He had been taking her out ever since and she was fond of him. But no more; she could not pretend. She teased him about his proposals, turned him down, lectured him on looking for another more suitable girl, and then proceeded to enjoy his company for another year.

Being the end of October, it was already dark and Beth had a last look round the shop, put the lights off and locked up. She lived only five minutes away from the shop, which was in the main wide street of Orborough. A quick cut through and she was in a quiet street near the sea-front, where home was in a Victorian house which had been converted into two flats. It was small, but very comfortable and very convenient, and for Orborough, the rent was not excessive.

That evening while she was making her holiday preparations, Beth found herself thinking of the work she hoped to do that winter. Through some friends, she had heard that Lord Tomlin of Haversham Hall was looking for someone to clean and restore his collection of paintings in the hall. Wondering if it was work that could be done in the space of the few months of winter, she had been trying to pluck up courage to ring up Lord Tomlin and ask him about it. She had met him in the shop where he came to look at, and occasionally to buy a painting. They had talked about the paintings at the hall, and she knew from what he had told her that the cleaning of the pictures would not be beyond her capabilities; she felt, in fact, that it would be a nice prospect for the winter and certainly a challenge.

Cases packed, she almost put her hand out to the phone to speak to Lord Tomlin about it, but at the last moment decided that it would be better if she waited until she came back from her holiday.

The next morning found her packing up the car to set off on her visit to an old schoolfriend, now married and living in the Lake District, complete with amiable husband, children and dogs.

Much as she loved the coast of East Anglia, she enjoyed the change and challenge of the hills and mountains and went prepared to do a lot of walking.

On the evening of her return from her holiday, Beth found a note from Dave at the flat to say that he would call round later that evening and take her out for a drink.

Beth was an arresting-looking girl; she dressed that night with care in a red needlecord dress which heightened the beauty of her long dark hair and her grey eyes. She had not seen Dave for more than a week and she found herself getting ready with a sense of excitement that surprised her.

He kissed her when he arrived and gladness and pleasure showed in his face.

"I've missed you, Beth," he said.

She laughed. "I've only been gone for a week," she replied.

"Are you dressed warmly?" he asked. "Put on your thickest coat; there is the loveliest of moons and it's quite still and I thought we could go for a walk along the beach first."

Beth did as she was told, and wound a long, woollen scarf around her head and neck.

Within minutes they could hear the crash of the waves over the pebbles and then the distinct, clear rattle as the water ran back.

They were the only ones out that cold still night, and it was when Beth loved the sea best. The moon shone on the water with startling clarity and the whole stretch of the beach was bathed in a soft silver glow, giving an eerie, unearthly feeling that only there, at that moment in time, did the night show such magical beauty.

Beth stopped at the water's edge, Dave's arm was close around her and she felt contentment, sensing that he felt as she did in the sound and sight of such a scene. Suddenly she gave a little shiver and he laughed gently at her.

"You're getting cold, come on, we'll go and find the warmth of the pub."

He had broken the spell but she knew he was right, "It seems a shame to go in," she said. "I don't know when I've seen it looking so lovely."

Their feet, crunching on the pebbles, made the only sound on that lonely shore and slowly they made their way back into the warm lights of the town.

Sitting in their favourite pub, Beth, looking at Dave, felt the excitement ebb just as the tide was ebbing, and once again she knew the feeling of safety and comfort that he gave her. He was very tall and very thin and the leanness in his looks gave his face a classic air of good-looking, fine intelligence. He smiled easily and laughter was never far from his eyes; she felt uneasily guilty that he was going to ask her a certain question, and in spite of the fact that she had been so pleased to see him, she knew that her answer would be the same. She felt foolish and she knew she was being foolish. No one would make a better or more loving husband than Dave, but another year had gone by and she was still hesitating. How stupid she was to let a secure affection slip her by in the hope that some day she might feel love for a man who would stir her senses, set her alight in a way that she could not feel for Dave. Were these the things of romantic novels? she thought. Or is true love in the safe feeling I have for Dave? Shall I ever know?

"Are you thinking about me, Beth?" Dave's smiling voice broke into her thoughts.

She met his eyes and she could see all the keen enthusiasm that his expression always held for her.

She did not speak and he put out his hand and took hers. "Beth, you have a faraway look that tells me that I am going to receive the same answer to my question. I wish I could think otherwise." He put both his hands round hers and gripped them tight. "I don't suppose you would marry me, would you, Beth? I do love you."

"Oh, Dave," there was genuine sorrow in her cry. "I can't say yes, I would like to but something always stops me. You will have to stop asking me, you know, find someone who will return love as it should be returned. Don't waste it on me."

He did not seem surprised, or even upset; he was grinning at her as though to tease her and lifted her hand to his lips.

"You never know, I might have found someone already," he said.

"What do you mean?" Beth asked,

intrigued by his tone and his expression.

"A new girl has started in the office this week, Margaret Benson, she likes to be called Polly for some reason. She's a stunner, very fair and very little; I quite fancy her."

Beth laughed and laughed. "Oh, Dave, you are never serious for long. I'll gladly stand aside for Polly, even if I've never met her. Perhaps she is the one."

"No one will ever hold a candle to you, Beth, but I've a feeling that somewhere out in the great wide world there must be a dynamic handsome hero who will come along and sweep you off your feet."

Beth was still laughing. "I can't imagine that ever happening, but I will let you know if it does. You ask your Polly out and I will be an interested bystander."

They walked home in a happy frame of mind, and Beth left him, feeling not quite so guilty as she usually did when she had turned him down. She would

11

pin her hopes on Polly.

The next thing Beth had to think about was contacting Lord Tomlin, and she soon found that she need not have worried about his reaction; he was enthusiastic, and the middle of that morning, she was in her car driving towards Haversham, a village between Orborough and Bury St Edmunds.

She thought about him as she drove along. He was a man now in his seventies, and lived in the village from which he had taken his title. He had been given a life peerage some years before, and Mr Robert Tomlin the wealthy industrialist had become Lord Tomlin of Haversham. He had bought Haversham Hall many years earlier at the time of his first marriage; he and his wife had spent much time and money refurbishing it from a sad state of dilapidation, and when she had died childless, he had been heartbroken. He did, however, re-marry and in his later years had two sons; Beth knew that his second wife had died recently and that his eldest son was married and shared the hall, while the youngest son lived and farmed at Haversham Farm. She had never met or seen either of them.

She stopped the car in the drive outside the front door of the hall and looked up at the house. The date 1675 was carved on the lintel and the building was as beautiful and as solid as its age implied.

Inside, she found herself standing in a large hall, shining and splendid in the dark oak of the wainscotting; her eye was caught instantly by a large and sombre landscape and she knew that if the other pictures were in the same state as this one, there was work to be done.

Then she saw a short grey-haired lady coming towards her, walking down a wide passage which was also hung with paintings.

"Miss Carrington?" She received a pleasant smile. "I am Mrs Pierce, Lord Tomlin's housekeeper; he is waiting for you in his room, perhaps you would

13

like to come with me."

Beth felt a little flutter of nerves as she followed Mrs Pierce. It was one thing to be selling Lord Tomlin a painting which he couldn't wait to possess, but another to be standing before him to be interviewed for a job.

She need not have worried.

Lord Tomlin was tall and burly, with a shock of white hair; he was smiling and he shook hands with her.

"Elizabeth." He had always called her Elizabeth, never the formality of Miss Carrington and neither the familiarity of Beth.

"I was very pleased to hear from you," he said. "But I hope that this does not mean that you are giving up the shop and the studio. We cannot do without you, you know."

Beth hastened to reassure him. "I always close for the winter, Lord Tomlin, so I'm not sure if that would give sufficient time to do the work. I have only the months from now until April free."

"Ah, yes, I had forgotten about the winter closing, but I don't think that will matter." He frowned for a moment, "I shall have to be honest with you. I have neglected my paintings; a lot of them were bought with the house and that was over thirty years ago, so you will understand that there is a lot of work to be done."

He had risen and was leading her to the door. "Before you come to any decision, you must see the library, that is where the majority of the pictures are hung," he said. "As far as I am concerned I cannot think of anyone better than you to do the task; you have the knowledge and the skill and I think you would be able to organize the work to get it finished over the winter. But I won't say any more, come and have a look."

Beth gave a gasp of delight when she saw the room, it was a library in the sense that there were glassfronted bookcases housing old leather-bound volumes; but there were pictures everywhere. Many were typical Victorian scenes, but there were others, small sketches and water-colours, landscapes and flower paintings in every available space.

Lord Tomlin was smiling at her. "Now you can see what needs doing there are more on the big landing upstairs; you can tell at a glance which ones require cleaning."

Beth was walking round the room thoughtfully, suddenly stopping and giving a loud exclamation. "Lord Tomlin, surely . . . surely this is a . . . "

He laughed out loud. "You have spotted it, clever girl, it is my Constable and it is my only valuable painting. Do you like it?"

Beth looked at the picture: it was not large but a perfect example of a Constable landscape, trees, river, meadow and sky; all bore the unmistakable stamp of the master.

"It is beautiful," she said. "Most of the others are later Victorian aren't they? You will be surprised at how different they will look once they are cleaned."

"I am not asking too much of you then?" he asked the eager girl.

Suddenly Beth looked at him and laughed in an excited way. "I can't resist it, Lord Tomlin; I would love to see these paintings in their original colours." He smiled in agreement. "I am looking forward to that, too," he said.

They discussed payment, which was generous and hours which he allowed to be completely flexible. She would start on Monday.

Beth left the room and walked down the corridor to the hall, her head in the clouds; she couldn't believe her luck. She was so wrapped up in her own thoughts that she did not notice the front door open and a man come into the hall. In her abstraction, she tripped over a rug and found herself saved from falling by the iron grip of someone's strong hands.

Startled, she looked up into angry

blue eyes in the face of a man who had more devastating good looks than anyone she had ever met. She was looking up a long way for he was tall; the brown hair was not distinguished but so carelessly worn and cut that it made his lean features seem almost aristocratic. But it was his eyes that held her, and then his voice, deep, incisive and at that moment, very angry.

"I suppose that you're a friend of Laura's, can't you look where you are going?" He glanced at her; something was upsetting him apart from this encounter and Beth did not reply.

His hands released their hold on her arms and without saying another word, he stalked off down the passage in the direction of Lord Tomlin's room.

She looked at his disappearing back, the autocratic, purposeful stride, the handsome head. He must be Lord Tomlin's eldest son, she thought; what a rude man, and I suppose Laura is his wife. No doubt I'll be seeing more of him, she said to herself, I think I'll try and keep out of his way.

She got into her car and drove back to Orborough highly pleased with herself, her mind filled partly with the sight of a roomful of paintings and partly with the impact of brilliantly angry blue eyes which she could not seem to forget.

2

ON the first day of the next week, Beth was in the library of Haversham Hall by 8.30 in the morning. She was keen, she was full of energy, and she had carefully unpacked her equipment and put it on a small table in the corner where it would be out of harm's way. She had a good look around at the pictures and decided to start on a rather heavy woodland scene which she felt must reveal hidden shades of green.

Mrs Pierce brought her coffee at mid-morning, but apart from the housekeeper, Beth saw no one until she had been there for three days. She normally worked until one o'clock, by this time feeling ready for lunch.

One morning, she was quietly concentrating, when she was surprised by a knock on the door and the appearance of a young woman in the room. Her long dark hair was knotted back, revealing a young face with large dark eyes. But when she spoke, Beth realized from her manner that she was older than she looked.

"Hello," said the stranger. "I've come to see how you are getting on, I couldn't believe it when Stephen said that the pictures were going to be cleaned professionally. I'm Laura, by the way."

"Laura?" Beth could not help the question in her voice.

"I don't suppose that anyone has explained the family to you. I'm Stephen's wife and James' mother, he's three years old, nearly four, and he's missing at the moment. We live in one half of the Hall. Grandad Tomlin had it converted when Grandma died, that was just after James was born." She stopped. "I'm talking a lot, aren't I? It's because I'm lonely. I don't even know your name."

"I'm Elizabeth Carrington, but I'm

always called Beth."

"Pleased to meet you, Beth," Laura held out her hand. "It's nice to see a young face around. And I must tell you that we have something in common; I'm an artist too, I'll tell you about it one day."

Beth shook hands; she liked the look of Laura. So this was the wife of the handsome stranger she had bumped into in the hall. They seemed rather an odd match.

Laura continued. "But I mustn't stop the good work or I'll have Grandad Tomlin after me; I'll come in one morning when it's coffee-time and we'll have a chat. I'm afraid I get bored and Stephen won't let me go out to work." She gave a smile and slipped out of the door.

Something seems wrong there, thought Beth: bored, lonely, didn't know where the little boy was; but she seemed nice, not pretty but a pleasant face, sensitive too.

She didn't see Laura again and on

the last morning of the week, she was suddenly aware of screaming and crying coming from outside her door. She got up hastily, but the door burst open and the handsome man she had assumed was Stephen Tomlin stood there and once again there was anger in his eyes. He was holding on to the small figure of a boy who was trying to pull away from him.

"I won't, I won't, I want to come with you," the child was yelling at the top of his voice.

He was suddenly lifted into the air and dumped down in front of Beth who looked both startled and bewildered.

"I don't know who you are," the irate man said, "but presumably you are helping Father. Well, if you are capable of cleaning a picture, I assume you are also capable of looking after an awkward three-year-old for a while. Laura can't be found and I haven't got time for him. Best of luck, I'll be back later." He stopped abruptly and stormed towards the door. "Just behave yourself. James."

And he was gone.

Beth started to breathe again; she had only met him twice and each time he had been rude and angry. But she had no time to think about this enigmatic man. She had to deal with a sobbing child who was lying on the floor at her feet, kicking and screaming. She had no experience of children whatsoever, she was always tense if customers brought them into the shop. And here she was with an unmanageable little boy left by his father and seemingly abandoned by his mother. Should she try and find Laura? she wondered.

She hastily put her cloths and solutions away and decided that the first priority was to try to calm this hysterical child.

She stood over him. "Hey you, what's your name?" she shouted at him.

There was a moment's stillness and she took advantage of it. "I'm Beth, what are you called?"

A mutter came from the figure on the floor: "James Robert Tomlin, Haversham Hall, Suffolk." She could just make out the words.

"Well, James Robert Tomlin, would you like to do some drawing with me?"

He did not reply, and sniffing, he sat up and looked round. She handed him a tissue and looked at his face; she could see a brightening of interest; had she succeeded?

As she was finding some pieces of paper, James began to talk. It didn't make a lot of sense, but there was a lot about Mummy and Cressida and someone called Maggie; Daddy was not mentioned very much, but Uncle Alex was. And as Uncle Alex seemed to be linked to the farm, she assumed him to be Lord Tomlin's younger son.

"What do you like playing with best, James?" she asked.

"Going on the farm," he replied.

"What about indoors, you can't always be on the farm?"

"Drawing," he said firmly. "And painting."

Beth heaved a sigh of relief and put the paper in front of him.

Then she found some pencils and a pen. "I haven't got any crayons," she said to him.

"I like pens best, Mummy doesn't let me have them."

Oh dear, thought Beth, I'll be in trouble with Laura, but I can't worry about that.

"Are you going to draw me something?"

But she needn't have spoken. Suddenly he was engrossed, crouched over the paper, drawing carefully, not the childish scribble she had expected.

He held the piece of paper up to her, it was a startlingly good drawing of a horse.

"Thank you, James, that's very good; can you do a dog?"

"Yes."

By lunch-time, they had gone all round the farmyard and half-way round the zoo; James was quite happy but there was no sign of his father. The boy was like him in looks, the dark brown hair and long thin face; he would be a good-looker one day, she thought.

It had been her intention to stay at the hall for the full day and she had brought some sandwiches and was going to beg a cup of coffee from Mrs Pierce. I suppose I'd better take James along to the kitchen, she thought, he must be hungry too.

At the moment she started to make a move, she turned sharply at the sound of someone coming into the room. The same handsome face and this time not angry, but smiling in a magnetic kind of way.

James rushed to him, "Uncle Alex, Uncle Alex," he cried out. "I've been drawing with Beth, come and see my pictures."

Beth stood frozen. The tall man was looking at her face with some amusement and then started to walk towards her.

"You . . . " she stammered. "I thought you were James' father, Laura's husband . . . I thought . . . "

Roars of laughter greeted her and she found her hand taken in his.

"God forbid that anyone should mistake me for Stephen, though I suppose we are alike superficially. And what gave you the idea that I was Stephen? I'd better introduce myself. Alexander Tomlin, farmer, better known as Alex."

They shook hands and Beth found herself shyly smiling. "Elizabeth Carrington, picture restorer, better known as Beth."

"And you thought I was the father of this little monkey?"

"Uncle Alex, I want to show you my drawings, I've done such a lot and Beth let me use a pen," interrupted the little monkey.

Alex Tomlin looked at her. "So you managed to calm him down, I take my hat off to you. Sorry I dumped him like that but I was desperate. We couldn't find Laura anywhere, and he'd come over to Maggie but she was busy. He loves to come round the farm with me but I was expecting someone from the Milk Marketing Board. Then I heard noises from the library and remembered that Father had got someone to do the paintings at last. I didn't realize it was you when I bumped into you last week; I'd just had a row with that blasted Cressida and I was in a temper. Come to think of it, I was in a temper this morning, too, wasn't I? That was Laura's fault. I shall have to make amends."

The conversation was doing nothing to enlighten Beth, and this Alexander Tomlin, obviously in a better mood, she felt she could put questions to.

"I'm sorry I thought you were Stephen, I knew there was another son but I didn't know his name. James kept talking about Uncle Alex, I think you are a hero to him or something. But can I ask you . . . I seem to be a bit confused, what with the things James has said," she stopped, hesitating. "Is Maggie your wife?"

More laughter came and he picked up James. "Tell Beth who Maggie is."

"Maggie is . . . Maggie."

Beth was indignant. "That tells me a lot. I don't think I shall ever sort your family out. I've met Laura and I know she's married to Stephen, and now I've met James, and you of course, but who is Maggie?"

"Maggie is my treasure," Alex said. "She comes to the farm every day; she's middle-aged and lovely and I love her, and she does all my cooking, all my cleaning and washing and generally runs my life. When she has time, she looks after James, he loves her too."

"So she's a kind of housekeeper. And Cressida, who is Cressida? She can't be your wife, unless you refer to your wife as 'that blasted Cressida'."

The smile faded.

"Cressida Blake is the daughter of our nearest neighbour and Father's closest friend, Samuel Blake; they live in the old rectory in the village. Cressida's mother was killed in a road accident when she was little and she has grown up very spoilt. Having said that, she is the most beautiful girl I have ever seen; she is nineteen and for the last five years at least, she has been convinced that she is going to marry me. In other words, she chases me, and nothing I say will penetrate her little bird-brain and persuade her otherwise. For your information, I am eleven years older than she is and a confirmed bachelor; I wouldn't off-load my temper on any woman, so you needn't cast your eyes in my direction, either."

Beth gasped. Bad temper, charm, conceit, what next was she going to discover in this aggravating man? What she was to find was a sense of the practical.

"Now I'm going to suggest that we all go across to the farm and have some lunch. Maggie will rustle up something. And if Laura hasn't appeared by that time, then James can stay with us this afternoon, and you can get on with your work."

For Beth, it was a hilarious lunch and also a revealing one; she came to know that Alex Tomlin was possessed of a sense of humour and a sense of fun, that he was kind, and that he had a great love of the things of nature. He was by instinct a good farmer and a man of the countryside.

She loved the farmhouse and would like to have had a good look round. It was built at the same time as the hall, but in contrast was a large, low sprawling building separated from the farm buildings by lawns and trees. The gardens were sheltered from the winds off the North Sea by a row of trees, which to Beth in their winter bareness looked like beeches.

She was almost reluctant to go back to work, but left James happily washing up in the kitchen with Maggie. Like most small children, he loved to help and it was a mystery to Beth why Laura was so neglectful of him. There was still no sign of her, but Alex said that she often took herself off when she got depressed and he was sure she would be back by tea-time.

By the end of the day, Beth had done what she had planned in spite of the interruptions. She was just finishing when she thought she heard the door open and looked up startled when she heard the sound of a voice; for a moment she thought it was Alex standing there except that it hadn't sounded like Alex. But the man coming into the library looked like a twin of Alex, except that he was heavier in build and was wearing black-rimmed spectacles.

She stood up and smiled at him. "Don't tell me, you must be Stephen. I can't be mistaken this time."

He shook hands with her and said gently, "You have the advantage of me, Miss . . ."

"Carrington, I'm Beth Carrington, I'm working on your father's pictures and I've already made the mistake of thinking that your brother Alex was you."

He put down the brief-case he was carrying and took off a dark businessman's raincoat. In his city suit, he walked around the library and looked at the painting she had been working on. "My goodness, what an improvement," he said. "I'm glad Father has found you; now tell me what has happened to cause you to mix me up with Alex. We're not really very alike."

His brother had said the same, mused Beth, but she wished she had not spoken as she was not sure how much she should tell him.

"I've been looking after James," she said, rather hesitatingly. "He's been in here drawing, oh and I'm afraid I let him use a pen, but it kept him quiet for over an hour . . ."

"Beth, I shall call you Beth, you are trying to evade the point. How did Alex come into it and where was Laura?" he asked grimly.

She told him then, and had to be honest and admit that she did not know if Laura had returned. James was all right, she had left him at the farmhouse with Maggie.

He bent towards her. "Thank you very much for helping out, we'll never be able to keep James away from you now, you suddenly seem to have become one of the family." Then he got up and started to put his coat on. "I'd better go and see if James is still with Maggie; I don't think I need look any further for Laura than the Old Rectory. She didn't know that I would be home early today; I work in the City, you know, sometimes I'm very late, but on a Friday I try and get away early if I can." He smiled at her. "Goodbye, Beth and thank you once again. I'm sure it won't be long before we meet again through the agency of young James."

After he had gone, Beth put her jacket on and made her way out to her car thinking what a strange day it had been. As she was unlocking the car door, another car was driven hastily across the front court and pulled up beside her. Curious, she did not get into her car and gave a start of surprise when she saw that it was Laura who was getting out of the other one.

"Beth," cried Laura. "Have you seen Stephen? I see his car is here. I didn't mean to be away for very long and now he is home before me and he is going to be furious. Or rather, Alex will be. Stephen doesn't lose his temper; he just goes quiet, which is even worse."

Beth walked across to her. "I'd better tell you," she said. "There's been an awful lot of trouble, where have you been?"

"Get in the car, we can't stand here in the cold. I'm so late a few more minutes won't hurt."

As Beth sat beside Laura, she felt she was being drawn further and further into the problems of this family.

Laura was speaking. "I left James with Maggie, I was sure he would be all right. He loves going to the farm, and I was only going to see Cressida for a few minutes."

Beth's thoughts broke into Laura's story; so Stephen had been right and Cressida had been involved.

"Cressida was on her way to Norwich to buy some clothes and begged me to go with her, she doesn't get much money but every penny is spent on clothes. She wants to be a model, but her father doesn't approve, so she hasn't got the money to pay for the training." Laura stopped and glanced through the dim light at the girl by her side, "That's beside the point. I don't know why I'm telling all this, but I took a liking to you and you seemed very sensible and trustworthy."

Beth grinned in the darkness, not the virtues one would wish to be remembered for, she thought, but went on listening.

"Well, we hunted for ages for what Cressida wanted. Every boutique in Norwich, even the Oxfam shop. Once she gets an idea into her head she has to have it; we found something in the end, in the market of all places, but she was dead pleased. We had a quick coffee and a sandwich and went back to the car, she's got a Mini. And it wouldn't start, no way. We had to call the AA, thank goodness her father made her join. But it seemed to take hours and I was getting more and more anxious. However, I'm home, and will have to face the consequences; tell me what has happened, is James all right?"

So Beth told her everything that had happened, including the fact that Alex had been angry, and that both men had thought she was somewhere with Cressida. They didn't seem to be really worried. James was at the farm all the afternoon, he was all right.

"Oh, you are a dear, fancy letting him do some drawing while you worked. I do love him you know, but some days it seems like an endless round of looking after a small child and I begin to wonder if there is anything else in life. Stephen doesn't understand, either; oh, I know I shouldn't be talking like this, but I'm afraid that Stephen and I seem to live under a cloud of continual disagreement."

3

WITH Laura's words ringing in her ears, Beth drove home as quickly as she could. She wanted to be alone, quiet, to sort out her thoughts; she was meeting Dave that evening and felt that she would like some time to think over all that had happened that day.

She absent-mindedly prepared and ate her meal and sat with her coffee by the fire until it was time to go and get changed.

Foremost in her mind was the last person she had spoken to and the centre of all the troubles of the day. Laura did not seem a happy person and Beth found this surprising. She had a lovely home, a clever and fascinating little boy, and as far as Beth could tell, a very nice husband. She had liked Stephen immediately; he raised none of the antagonism in her that his brother did and she felt she would like to know him better and to find out what was wrong between him and Laura — not just to hear Laura's side of the story.

Alex she thought of as an enigma; was he really a bad-tempered person or just short on patience? she wondered; she had a feeling that it might be the latter. He had shown her a different side to his character over the farmhouse lunch, and it was certainly a side that she could come to like a lot.

She was intrigued by the young Cressida and felt that it would not be long before she would meet her.

It was in fact, only a matter of two hours; she got ready and a cheerful Dave picked her up and they drove to a village pub half-way between Orborough and Haversham.

It was a light-hearted evening and Beth felt totally relaxed in Dave's company. She was watching his face as he talked to her when suddenly his expression changed and his voice tailed off into silence.

"Wow!" he exclaimed, his tone and his face full of awe and a gleeful appreciation of something unusual. "There's the kind of man that I said would do for you, Beth, and just look at that girl, she must be straight out of Hollywood."

Beth turned slightly, so as not to appear rude, and her heart gave a sudden lurch as she saw, standing by the bar, no less a figure than Alex Tomlin, in casual clothes and designer sweater; he was catching all eyes, as was the girl who stood by his side laughing up at him.

Was it, Beth thought, could it be Cressida? She was dressed stunningly all in white except for long black boots and a vivid red scarf worn casually around her shoulders; her hair fell straight almost to her waist, not just fair, but beautifully corn-coloured and shiny. Her features were even and perfect, dominated by glowing eyes of the deepest blue. No wonder that Dave had been stopped in mid-speech, thought Beth ruefully.

At that moment, before she had time to turn back to Dave, Alex looked away from the girl at his side and his eyes met those of Beth. She was certain she was colouring in her embarrassment, but then realized somewhat to her delight, that pleasure showed in Alex's eyes as he recognized her. Immediately, he took the girl's arm and urged her towards Beth's table.

"Beth, fancy meeting you again today and here of all places. May I introduce Cressida Blake to you?" His eyes held a wicked glint and Beth had the feeling that he was urging her to think of this girl as 'that blasted Cressida'.

But she did not allow herself to be disturbed by his teasing manner and got up and introduced Dave.

Alex asked to join them. Dave looked pleased enough but there was no pleasure on Cressida's face. She looked cool and superior, but beneath

Alex's eyes she obviously decided that she must show herself at her best and try to impress.

Afterwards, Beth could only think of the evening with amusement; the two men got on well from the start, finding the property market, and particularly the agricultural property market, a topic they both enjoyed talking about. Beth sat and listened, trying to hide the inner chuckles she felt at the peeved look on Cressida's face.

At last, feeling sorry for her, Beth let it be known that Laura had told her about the expedition to Norwich and with the attention turned towards herself, Cressida was all smiles again.

As they parted Alex made it clear that he was pleased to have met Beth and Dave and even hinted at another meeting.

Dave laughed as he started up the car. "I like your boyfriend, Beth . . . "

"He's not my boyfriend and you know it, Dave Nelson."

"Oh, Beth, I'm only teasing you, but

I don't think you'd get a look in with young Cressida around. She's got her hooks into him and no mistake. Did you see her face when he suggested that they joined us?"

"I think she's very spoilt from what Alex told me and Laura said that she wants to be a model but her father won't let her." Beth did not know why she was trying to defend Cressida.

"I would have thought that she could have twisted any man round her little finger," said Dave sardonically.

"But you need money to go modelling and Mr Blake is not forthcoming. I think she plagues Alex rather."

"Well, I can't say I'd mind being plagued by someone as lovely as Cressida Blake," Dave laughed.

"Dave Nelson, you are a womanizer!" Beth laughed too. "Here you are, taking me out for the evening, talking about Cressida and no doubt there's Polly in the offing as well."

"There's safety in numbers, you know, and you are to blame in any case, young Beth."

"Oh, Dave, you are good for me; I was really bothered by the set-up at Haversham Hall, but it all seems in perspective now, especially after meeting Alex with Cressida. I'm glad I've met her."

After the troubles of that particular day, things seemed to settle down at Haversham Hall. Beth worked hard and Lord Tomlin seemed pleased at the progress she was making. During those weeks, she did not see Alex at all and very little of Laura. But one person she did see regularly and she began to look forward to Friday afternoons when she was clearing up at the end of the week; Stephen came home early from the City and got into the habit of bringing James to see her.

She always had pencils and crayons and plenty of paper ready, and James was quite happy to sit and draw while Beth and his father had a chat.

Stephen spoke very little about Laura and gave no intimation that all was not well between them until one day just before Christmas. The conversation started with no hint that anything was disturbing him.

"You love doing this, don't you, Beth?"

She looked at him, sensing that he was asking the question seriously and with a particular purpose.

"Yes, I do, Stephen, and I've been lucky being able to work here."

Then he changed the subject abruptly. "And what about if you got married, Beth, would you give up the shop and all this?"

As Beth had often thought over this particular hypothetical question herself, she had no difficulty in answering, but she still felt that it was strange for Stephen to be talking in this way. He spoke in a troubled fashion as though fighting with some inner problem and she imagined that he must somehow be trying to relate her feelings to his own marriage.

"I can't be sure, can I?" she replied.

"But I've always thought that I would like to keep on the shop until the time came to start a family; then devote a few years to the children until the time came when I felt I could open a shop again. But these are all 'ifs' Stephen, as I haven't got a husband and I can't be sure what he would want if I did. I suppose I'm old-fashioned, really; a lot of career women want to continue working and hand the children over to a grandparent or a nanny or something." She looked at him, his expression had not changed and she had no idea if she had helped him in his difficult thoughts. "I happen to believe that the first two or three years of a child's life are important enough for a mother to be the best person to look after the child. But it's not always that easy, some women get bored and irritable and that's just as bad for the children as if she was out at work." She seemed to be saying rather a lot and he did not interrupt. "Above all, it's something that each family, each couple must decide for themselves, there just cannot be the same rule for everyone."

Suddenly he smiled and leaned forward and touched her hand. "Thank you, Beth, I knew you would give me a straight answer. Bless you. I think things have been easier since you came, I enjoy coming to see you on a Friday afternoon and James wouldn't miss coming. When I get home, the first thing he says is 'Are we going to see Beth?'"

Beth was glad of the change of subject and they admired James' drawings.

Stephen left her then and she quietly pondered his words; she wondered if she would ever hear more of Laura's side of the story. It was not something she could very well ask, even though Laura seemed friendly and pleased to come in for coffee from time to time.

She saw nothing of Alex and felt a slight sense of disappointment after the friendliness of the evening when she had met him with Cressida. She even wondered if Cressida had anything to do with it.

Time went quickly and at Christmas she took two weeks off to go and visit her parents in north Norfolk. She enjoyed the break but at the end of the holiday she found herself glad to be at work again. After the quietness of the weeks before Christmas, the new year brought a string of happenings which brought Beth into the heart of the complications of family life at Haversham Hall.

On her first day back, Beth was pleased to see Laura in the library at mid-morning and thought immediately that there was some change in her. Laura had often worn a worried expression previously, but now she was tense and strained, her fingers plucked nervously at the woollen cuff of her jacket and she didn't greet Beth as she came into the room.

"Happy New Year, Laura," said Beth, and then regretted her words.

"Thank you, Beth, I expect it will

be for you. As far as I'm concerned, there's nothing happy about it nor likely to be."

Beth was taken aback at the venom in the words and did not know how to respond. But she didn't need to say anything as Laura seemed to have come with the purpose of sharing her troubles.

"I've got to talk to someone, Beth, do you mind? Cressy doesn't seem to want to know, she's so wrapped up in her own problems." Laura looked at her and Beth could see the tears brimming in her eyes as she went on speaking. "Stephen doesn't seem to understand, I don't think I can stand much more. He says my place is with James, not back at work in an art studio, which is really what I'd love to do. I suppose the trouble is that he just doesn't take the painting seriously, he doesn't see it as a career. Just as though I was dabbling around for a bit of fun." She broke off and her hand wiped away a tear. "He doesn't understand how important it is to me, we will never agree, not ever and I don't know what to do."

Beth felt embarrassed at Laura's outpourings, but felt a reply was expected of her.

"Laura, isn't it possible for you to paint here at Haversham Hall? Have your own studio or something?"

Laura shook her head. "No, I tried it, but the problem was James, as he got older he was always into things and I couldn't concentrate. It just didn't work."

Beth was remembering the conversation she had had with Stephen and the questions he had asked her. She realized now that she had not helped Laura's cause when she had spoken her own thoughts to him.

Then Laura suddenly burst out: "Beth, you often see Stephen, I know he brings James every week. Could you say something to him? He might take notice of you, I know he likes you."

"But Laura," objected Beth. "I can't

interfere in your marriage. It wouldn't be right. Can't you think of it as only being a short while longer? After all, I expect James will soon be going to nursery school."

"I know, I've thought of that, but I feel so desperate. It's a kind of post-natal depression come very late. But I must not worry you, it's been great to talk to you. Thank you, Beth."

"I'm afraid I've been no help at all," said Beth. "But I do hope that things will improve for you. Come any time you feel like it, Laura, sometimes it helps just to talk, doesn't it?"

"Yes, it does, you are quite right. I feel a bit better already. I'll go and fetch James from Maggie, she is so good with him, but she is a busy person, I'm afraid I impose on her."

Laura left her, giving Beth a lot to think about; she had no idea how she could help but she would like to have seen a happier situation between Stephen and Laura for James' sake.

The extent to which James was being

neglected by his mother was brought home to Beth the very next day. She was working quietly in the library, when she was suddenly disturbed by the door being opened violently and the shrill sound of her name being called.

Turning sharply, she saw to her amazement an agitated Cressida coming up to her. She had not seen the girl since the night in the pub and had assumed that she was not in favour because Cressida had lost Alex's sole attention that evening.

"Beth, I'm sorry, I shouldn't have burst in like that when you're working but I didn't know what to do," the distracted Cressida cried out. "I've lost James."

Beth got up and was inclined to be scornful. "Lost James? How can you possibly have lost him . . . ?"

"You don't understand. It's all my fault, I was looking after him for Laura, she's gone to Bury for some paints and . . . well, I was trying out some new make-up and I forgot James for a moment. I thought he was drawing, he was so quiet, but when I looked round he had disappeared. I've looked everywhere in the house but he's nowhere to be found. What shall I do?" Cressida was wailing pathetically and Beth felt like shaking the beautiful but silly girl.

"Just stop making such a fuss and let's think," she said in exasperation, and Cressida was struck dumb, as though no one had ever spoken to her in such a fashion before. "The most likely thing that James would do is to go over to the farm, have you been to ask Maggie if she has seen him?"

Cressida shook her head. "No, I didn't think of that. I didn't think that he would go out of the house."

Beth took her by the arm. "Well, let's lose no time. We'll go and find Maggie first."

They almost ran out of the hall and down the lane that led to the farmhouse. Beth's heart sank when they got there; at the back, the outside kitchen door was shut up and there was no sign of Maggie. Was it possible that James might have wandered into the farmyard or even into the fields?

They called and called him, but there was not only no sign of James, there was no sign of life at all. Tractors and machines were lying still and idle on the cold January day.

Still holding Cressida's arm, Beth led the way through an open gate into a field green with the first blades of winter wheat.

Then she stopped and clutched at Cressida's hand. "Look," she said, and pointed to a path at the side of the field.

Walking hurriedly and pulling a sobbing James behind him was an irate Alex. He slowed down when he saw them, but even from that distance they could see the black expression of anger on his face.

"What the hell is going on?" he shouted. "I found James wandering along the field; you know he's not allowed in the fields on his own, no child is; it's too dangerous when we've got the machinery out and the ditches are full in winter. What are the two of you thinking about? And where is Laura?"

4

THEY stood confronting one another and it was James who broke the taut and angry silence. "Beth," he cried. "Beth." And tearing himself from Alex's grasp, he threw himself into Beth's arms. "Maggie wasn't there and I only wanted to go to the jungle. But the jungle has gone as well. Uncle Alex is cross with me."

She held him close, not knowing what he was saying, except that it was an unalterable fact that Alex was cross. But as she bent her head towards James, she saw Cressida moving towards Alex. The next moment she was being held in a close embrace. "Oh, Alex, thank goodness you found him. I was so worried when Beth said he might have gone into the fields."

Cressida was a tall girl but Alex looked down on her and he stroked

58

her golden hair and murmured her name.

At the same time, his blazing eyes met those of an outraged Beth. "So you let him stray, did you, while you were concentrating on your damned pictures? I suppose Laura left him with you for a few minutes and look what happens. Luckily he's come to no harm."

Beth was struck dumb at his words; not only was he making the wrong assumption and was venting his anger on her, but the silent Cressida was clinging to him, her head buried in his shoulder, letting Beth take the blame for what she had done.

Beth didn't often lose her temper, but this time, in the cold wind of a gaunt East Anglian field, she saw red and felt the heat of her rage rise up in her.

She thrust James towards Alex and turned away, shouting shrilly as she started to run back down the path. "You look after him then, if you're so good at it. I've really had enough of your family. I'll stick to my painting in future."

She realized as she ran that her words implied that she was guilty of losing James. But she did not care, every time she met Alex Tomlin he lost his temper, with the one exception when he went all out to charm in front of Dave.

As for Cressida, she could not believe the perfidy of the girl. It was so imperative for her to stay in Alex's good books, that she had happily stayed silent while Beth received the abuse from him, and she had revelled in the comfort and closeness of the man she sought so desperately.

Back in the library, Beth hastily cleared up and made her way home. Her anger was slow to cool and it was not like her. Why should she be so upset because Alex thought badly of her? she asked herself. She hardly knew the answer; as far as she could think back over the three or four times that she had met him, on each occasion tensions had run high. She had had glimpses of a different Alex but they were rare, and she wished she could forget the brilliant angry eyes of an hour ago; she could not even bring herself to acknowledge that his temper had been out of his concern for his little nephew. Cressida Blake stood between her and all that, and as far as she was concerned, Alex was welcome to a vain and devious Cressida, however beautiful she might be.

That evening, seeing Alex's face instead of Wogan's on TV, remembering almost with hatred the deception of Cressida, Beth could not settle to anything. She even thought of giving Dave a ring, but she had not seen a lot of him since before Christmas; however, she decided she must talk to someone and on her way to the phone, she was pulled up short by a sharp rap on her front door. Perhaps by some miracle it is Dave, she said to herself as she went to open the door,

When she saw who was standing there, she was speechless. Alex Tomlin, tall and as dynamic as ever, in a thick waterproof jacket, looking at her with an expression which was incomprehensible, "Alex . . . " she faltered and did not even make a move to ask him in.

He did not wait to be asked; he took her by the arm, closed the door behind him, and stood in her living-room looking down at her.

"Don't say anything, Elizabeth Carrington, get a warm coat and a woolly scarf or something and come with me, I have something to say to you . . . "

Beth found her voice. "But I don't have anything to say to you, Mr Alexander Tomlin; after what you thought this afternoon, I'm surprised you've got the nerve to seek me out. And how did you know where I lived in any case?"

He took no notice of her waspish tone. "It is because of this afternoon I want to speak to you, and I got your address from Father, that wasn't difficult. And I want to take you somewhere, so go and get ready; oh, and you'd better put thick shoes on as well. It's not a night-club I'm taking you to."

His tone, his eyes, his manner were compelling and Beth had not the strength to deny him. And she did not want to, she found that she wanted to talk to him if only to relieve her pent-up feelings.

He had the Range Rover at the front of her flat and she got in and sat by his side without saying a word. He did not speak either and drove down country lanes as though he had been on a main road; Beth did not lose her sense of direction, she knew the lanes as well as he did. It was after they had left a sleepy Westleton and turned off the Dunwich Road that words were forced out of her.

"This road only goes to Dunwich Cliff," she said.

"I know."

She said no more and she waited for him to slow down as they reached the car-park, dark and deserted on a winter's night.

She climbed out and as they walked from the car, Beth found that it wasn't completely dark. Clouds raced in the sky, hiding the moon, but giving light to the sea and the shore. She knew these paths, it was one of her favourite places and the track along to the Minsmere hides was straight and easy. She shivered as they met the south-east wind head-on, and her companion's arm came round her shoulders. She shivered again, this time at his touch, but was glad of the warmth.

As much as she loved this part of the world, Beth had never been here after dark, nor would she have thought it the ideal place for the kind of conversation they must have.

She was getting colder and colder in

spite of their brisk pace and at last she spoke. "How far are we walking?" she asked.

"As far as the hide," was his reply.

She looked at him in astonishment. "The hide? But you can't go in the hide after dark, you won't see a thing."

Along the shore, where the boundaries of Minsmere Bird Reserve lay, were one or two small hides used by bird-watchers who did not go to the Reserve itself. Beth had been there many times in daylight hours.

"Wait and see, Beth, you will be surprised, and we will be out of the wind and you can listen to what I have to say."

I'm not the only one who's going to do the listening, she thought fiercely, and tramped along at his side with a strange feeling of happiness that was somehow mixed up with her resentment.

The hide was not locked and Alex took the shutter down as they settled themselves on the hard wooden bench.

Out of the wind, it felt warm and Beth also felt a warmth from his very nearness.

He did not speak and she realized that he was looking out as intently as if he had held a pair of binoculars trained on the avocets. She followed his gaze and was astonished; the hidden moon gave a grey and ghostly light and in spite of the darkness, she could see the reeds bending before the wind like phantoms. There were ripples on the water where there were usually birds and the whole scene caught her in a magic spell. Beyond the water and the reed beds, she could pick out the shapes of the trees where in the summer she had watched the marsh harrier fly in and out of the green foliage.

It was not even quiet; she recognized the owls and thought she caught a glimpse of them on their nocturnal flight, but there were other nameless night birds adding to the ghostliness of the bewitching scene.

Alex moved closer to her and tried to see her face.

"Well, what do you think? You've not been here at night-time before?" he asked her.

"No, I would never have thought of it. It is like a different world; even the reeds seem to have a life of their own," she replied.

"I knew you wouldn't let me down, Beth," he said softly.

The personal remark sparked off memory of the earlier events of the day in her.

"You don't know anything about me," she retorted. "You even . . . " But she was not allowed to finish what she was going to say.

"No, Beth, I've brought you here for a special reason and I want to get it right."

He took her hand in his and drew it nearer to him. "I lost my temper with you this afternoon, Beth, and I've got to apologize to you."

"Apologize? You mean you know

what happened?"

"Yes, I do," he said. "And all I can say is that I'm sorry. I did you a great injustice. I thought it was you who had been left in charge of James, didn't I?"

"So Cressida told you." Beth felt a sense of relief that the grudge she had harboured against Cressida was not justified.

"Cressida?" His voice was a question; he knew his Cressida. "No, she waited for her kiss, left me to take James back to the farmhouse and then she went home."

"But . . . ."

"Laura told me, Beth. She returned very soon afterwards and came looking for us. She guessed that James would have asked to go to the farm." He held her hand close in both of his. "I know now that it was Cressida who was left in charge of James, and that he must have slipped out when she wasn't looking. She was probably doing her hair or something."

For the first time, Beth laughed, it was so near to the truth.

And it broke the tension between them. She told him just what had happened and how relieved she had been to see James safely with him.

"But Alex, there was something James said; he said he wanted to go to the jungle but it wasn't there; what did he mean?"

It was Alex's turn to laugh and she was glad to hear it. "It was in the summer," he said, "and James remembered. That field was full of broad beans and they were so tall, that when we walked along the path they were right above his head, and there was a lot of hogweed too, so he was just dwarfed. He thought it was a great game crawling through it, we pretended we were tigers in the jungle."

"Oh, Alex," Beth smiled in delight; this handsome, autocratic man was showing a very different side to his character. "You love James."

"Yes, I do love James, I think he's a great lad."

She could sense the worry behind the simple statement and voiced her thoughts. "And you worry about him?"

Alex glanced in her direction. "You know, then," he said. "Yes, I do worry about him, but I don't know what to do about it. Does Laura talk to you?"

"Yes, she does and Stephen, too," she said and regretted the words as soon as they were out.

"Stephen talks to you? I don't believe it. He's the most reserved person I've ever met, you must have made a hit with him. When on earth do you have the opportunity to speak to him? Not meeting him on the sly, I hope."

Beth was furious. "Alex Tomlin, that was completely uncalled for. Why should you think something like that?"

"I'm sorry," he said. "It's just that knowing Steve, I can't imagine him telling his troubles to anyone."

Beth told him about the Friday

70

afternoons; she did not want to quarrel with him.

"It's hopeless, isn't it?" He looked at her. "But it's James I feel sorry for; he is pushed everywhere, to Cressida, to Maggie, and look what's happened today. Can you see a solution, Beth?"

"That's the trouble," she answered. "I seem to be able to see both sides of the story. If it were me, I feel I would want to be with my child when he's at such a fascinating age, so I think Stephen feels that I'm sympathetic towards him; but on the other hand a lot of women keep on a career these days, so I can see Laura's point of view. What would you do if it was your wife, Alex?"

He laughed. "You forgot I told you that I was forever a bachelor, in spite of what Cressida thinks, but I really don't think that a child comes to any harm with a nanny or nursemaid or whatever, if it means he has a happier mother and father. I think the very worst thing for James must be the strained relations

71

between Stephen and Laura. But there, we none of us know what we would do in the same circumstances, so I don't feel we can sort out their lives for them. I do what I can for James and I know he loves the farm. I'm not sure if he'll be a farmer or an artist when he grows up!"

Beth smiled and was relieved at the change of tone. "He certainly spends a lot of his time drawing animals, he is very talented isn't he?"

"Yes, I think he's very advanced for his age. Most children of his age would draw a round for a head, with four sticks coming out of it for arms and legs and say that was Mummy."

They laughed together and Beth felt Alex's arm come round her shoulders.

"Am I forgiven?" he asked her.

"Yes, it was a misunderstanding after all," she replied.

"Do I get a kiss, then?" His fingers came under her chin as he said the words and before she had time to speak, his mouth was on hers, a simple light pressure of his lips; and in her surprise she did not move away. Taking her quietness for assent, he pulled her towards him and the kiss deepened until both felt a thrill of contact that kept them close for a long time.

At last, Alex lifted his head and framed her face with his hands; it was a gentle gesture. "If you are going to kiss me like that," he joked, "I shan't remain a confirmed bachelor for long."

And he got up and still holding her close to his side, he managed to do up the shutter and open the door of the hide. The cold east wind met them with a blast, and they half ran along the track to the cliff and the shelter of the car.

They were silent on the way home, but it was a silence of friendliness, and when they parted, Alex seemed to have only one thing to say.

"Thank you, Beth, I'm glad that we sorted things out between us. I'd better not say that I'll see you again or I'll have Dave on my tail."

"And Cressida, too," she added and they said a cheerful good-night and Alex was on his way.

Beth let herself into the flat half-bemused; it had all been unexpected and unusual; the magic of Minsmere had been reflected in the magic of a kiss, and it was an evening she was not going to forget in a hurry.

She went to Haversham Hall next day, wondering if she would have a visit from Cressida, but the morning passed and she worked quietly on her own. She had finished the pictures in the library and had started to bring the paintings from the entrance hall and the long corridor one by one; she was quite pleased with her progress and so was Lord Tomlin and she was confident that she would finish the work before Easter.

Beth finished at lunch-time that day and made her way to the car; as she reached the big gates, she was surprised to see Cressida walking towards the hall. As usual her clothes looked more suited to the London salon than the Suffolk countryside and when Cressida realized that it was Beth in the car, she started to wave her arms wildly.

Beth parked outside the gates and got out of the car to speak to the girl. She was not overkeen to see Cressida, wishing to put the incident behind them, but she supposed that Cressida might want to apologize to her.

But afterwards she smiled at this idea and thought that it was not in Cressida's nature to apologize to anyone.

"Beth, I was just coming to see you. I thought you worked in the afternoons." The young girl was friendly and Beth joined her in the shelter of the trees just inside the gates of the hall.

"It varies from day to day," Beth replied. "And also how the work is going. I wanted an early day today."

"I won't keep you," Cressida smiled. "I wanted to talk to you about Alex."

Beth was silent, remembering the

charm of the previous evening with Alex. What was Cressida going to say?

"I know that Alex was cross with you yesterday," said Cressida, "but I've a feeling he likes you and I just wanted to tell you how things stood between Alex and me."

Beth could not speak, the gall of this girl. Certainly no apology for putting her in the wrong with Alex over James' disappearance; this sounded more like a hands-off warning. She felt like getting straight back into the car and driving off, but Cressida was still speaking and her words caught Beth's attention.

" . . . and even when I was small, Alex said he would marry me when I grew up." Cressida stopped speaking, and her look seemed to be to gauge the effect of her words on Beth. "I know I've still got to train, I'm going to be a model, you know. But Alex will wait for me, I know he loves me; he wouldn't make love to me if he didn't, would he?"

Beth focussed on Cressida with a start. Whatever was the girl saying? It certainly wasn't the picture of Alex's feelings for Cressida that she had received; he had implied that Cressida was a nuisance to him. Was he amusing himself with the lovely young girl?

It somehow didn't seem in character.

That Cressida was devious, Beth knew, but what she was saying sounded sincere and had a youthful hope.

"And do you love Alex?" she found herself asking Cressida.

"I adore him," was the reply. "He's the most good-looking man I've ever met. But I want to go to model school before I get married. I'm still working on Daddy to let me go. I wish it wasn't so expensive, you would never believe how much it costs and then you have to live in London."

Beth couldn't help herself when she spoke next, she hardly had patience with Cressida, but to a certain extent she was intrigued by the girl's plans and her connection with Alex.

"But, Cressida," she said, and she was being thoughtful. "Once you are a model, however are you going to fit in modelling and being a farmer's wife? If you don't mind me saying so, the two hardly seem to mix?"

Cressida laughed. "I've thought it all out; Alex will buy me a flat in London and I shall come back to Haversham at weekends. He's busy all hours of the week in any case, I would hardly see him so he wouldn't mind. I think he will be pleased for me to have a career. Not like . . . " She stopped suddenly and Beth knew that she had been going to say not like Laura.

But it was obvious she didn't want the conversation to stray from herself. "I love Haversham Farm," she said. "It's a beautiful old house and just lends itself to modernization."

Beth gave an involuntary shudder, this was one of the most ridiculous conversations she had ever had, and she was a sudden thought. "What about children, Cressida? Won't you want a family?" she asked and wasn't surprised at the reply she recieved.

She broke off what she was saying, and started to wave her arm. "Oh, look, Beth, here is Alex. How funny we should just be talking about him. He can give me a lift up to the farm."

The Range Rover came to a sudden halt inside the gates and Alex jumped out. He was smiling and as he looked in Beth's direction, she had the feeling that the smile was meant for her.

But it was Cressida who claimed his attention and held on to his arm.

"What's all this?" he said. "Having a girlish gossip?"

"I'm just going home," said Beth.

"Oh, I'm sorry, I thought I might see you later on this afternoon. Never mind, tomorrow will do."

Cressida's face began to lose its smile as Alex was speaking to Beth.

But Alex looked down at her. "Don't look so serious, Cressy love. Come on, jump in and we'll go and get some lunch."

Beth watched the look of triumph on Cressida's face as the girl got into the Rover without saying goodbye.

She walked back to the car and drove home furiously, seeing first Alex's face and then Cressida's and unable to believe the truth of Cressida's words or to forget that last look on her face. Cressida might as well have said, 'I told you so', before she drove off with Alex.

5

THAT evening, Beth was going out with Dave, but all the time she was getting ready she was thinking of Alex. I seem to be seeing three different men rolled into one, she thought. There was the Alex of the short temper and the angry eyes; there was the Alex of Minsmere, pleasant, sincere and able to rouse her with his kisses; and now she had this picture of a different Alex. Was all that Cressida had said just fancy? She had seemed so serious and so convinced that Alex cared for her, planning a future which included him and trying to convince Beth that Alex returned her feelings.

Beth could not help the doubts; the Alex she had come to know just did not fit the picture that Cressida had drawn. Or, and her thoughts faltered painfully, was there really another Alex who would kiss one girl one night, and at the same time lead another to think of marriage?

She tried to dismiss the enigmatic Alex Tomlin from her mind and concentrate on the thought of an evening with Dave. It was the first time she had seen him since before Christmas and she looked forward to an evening of uncomplicated and pleasant conversation.

But half-way through the evening, Beth realized that Dave seemed preoccupied, as though he had something on his mind.

"What is it, Dave? Is something worrying you? I asked you something and you didn't reply."

He put his hand across the table and covered her own. "I'm sorry, Beth, but you are right. There is something I have to tell you and I just don't know how."

She looked at him, the sensible, reliable face she had known and liked these last years; could she guess what he was going to say?

He did not speak and she said gently, "Is it Polly?"

"Oh, Beth," he said with some distress. "How did you know?"

She grinned. "Sixth sense, I think. I know you liked her even if you joked about it."

"I'll have to be honest," he said. "We just fell for each other. I was with her at the firm's Christmas dinner and took her home afterwards and that was that. But I feel such a fool, Beth, there was I asking you to marry me every few months and the next girl I meet I go and fall in love with."

Beth smiled at him. "Ours was a good friendship, Dave. I know it was no more than that or we would have been married ages ago. I am very pleased for you, and I hope you'll be very happy together."

"Thank you, Beth, it's not got as far as that. I couldn't say anything to Polly until I had seen you. I wondered if we could all go out one evening, I would like you to meet her," he said.

"Oh, Dave," Beth laughed. "Polly won't want to meet me."

"Yes, she will," he interrupted. "I've told her about you, I hope you don't mind. I want her to know how nice you are and not a threat to our happiness."

"All right then, if you put it like that. I'd love to meet her."

They said good-night and Beth went home with a sense of sadness, though she was very pleased for Dave's sake. It was a selfish feeling, she would miss him so much and there would be many lonely evenings.

But she was to find that working at Haversham Hall, amongst the Tomlin family, gave her more than enough to do and certainly enough to think about. She guessed that Alex was seeing a lot of Cressida but he also came into the library on occasions to see her, just as Stephen did. One morning he arrived with a cheerful smile and a suggestion which pleased Beth very much.

"Working hard, Beth?" he asked as

he came in the door. "I've just popped in to ask you something. When the weather is better what do you say to taking James to Minsmere, just the two of us? Don't you think he would love it there?"

Beth looked at him; she almost felt like asking him what Cressida would say, but she could not.

"It's a great idea, Alex, I'd love to go, but do you think James is old enough?"

"Yes, I do; he'd love to run along the beach in any case and I think he would like looking for birds from the hide, judging by his interest on the farm."

"Yes, that's true, we're sure to have a nice sunny day sometime in January, it's not always cold and windy."

"Good," said Alex. "That's settled then. I'll ask Laura and the first fine day we'll go. I hope it's not too far away, Beth, I shall look forward to it."

She said goodbye to him, and sat

down thinking after he had gone. He's so nice sometimes, she said to herself, I just wish he wasn't so complicated, it would be so easy to like him.

Beth was to bite back her words a few days later. Stephen came on Friday as usual and James brought a new jigsaw to show Beth. It was a circular one and was made up of birds and animals in a woodland setting. James loved it and was as quiet as a mouse, patiently fitting the pieces together.

Stephen looked sadly at him and Beth did not know what to say. They were standing in the French window and James would not be able to hear what they were saying if they kept their voices low.

"He's always on his own, poor little chap," Stephen said. "And the way things are going, I don't suppose he'll ever have a brother or a sister."

Beth was startled, it was not like Stephen to say something so intimate.

"We've had another quarrel, Beth, Laura and I. She doesn't seem like the

Laura I first knew, I wish I understood her."

Beth knew she would have to make a reply and felt awkward and embarrassed.

"Laura is an intelligent girl, Stephen, she needs something to keep her mind occupied," she started to say.

"I know all that," said Stephen. "But surely she could be teaching James and taking him out and about more? There is so much for a child of his age to learn and I think it is best learned from his mother."

Beth sighed; the two seemed as far apart as ever on this thorny subject. She glanced at James but he was completely absorbed in his jigsaw and not taking any notice of what his elders were saying.

"Perhaps it will be better when James is at school," she offered, but Stephen was gloomy.

"That's nearly eighteen months away, and it will be too late then."

"Stephen, don't talk like that. Look,

is there any way I can help? Could I look after James for a weekend or something while you and Laura have a break together, a short holiday; perhaps that's what you need."

Beth was in earnest, and Stephen took his gaze away from the view out of the window and looked down at her.

"You are very kind, Beth, sometimes I think you save my sanity. But it's no good, we aren't even speaking to each other at the moment."

Beth groaned. "And you are two intelligent people," she said. "But the offer's there and I mean it. I would do anything I could to help you."

His arm came round her and he dropped a kiss on the top of her head.

"Bless you," he said and then jerked his head round quickly at the sound of an angry voice from the doorway.

"What the hell is going on here?" said an irate Alex as he walked into the room. "I had a suspicion that there was something between the two of you and it looks as though I'm right."

Stephen went over and gathered up James, who screamed at being forced to leave his jigsaw, and confronted his brother. "Beth and I have been having a chat and it's no business of yours," he said shortly and strode out of the room with a kicking James.

Beth was still standing in the window, almost turned to stone at the scene which had just taken place.

Alex shut the door with a loud slam and stood before her. She had seen his eyes blazing with anger before, but it was nothing to the explosive expression in them now; it held not only anger, but hurt and a grasping to understand what he had just witnessed.

"Are you playing fast and loose with my brother just when his marriage is in great difficulties?" he shouted at her, and his hands went out and grasped her arms.

At the feel of his tight grip on her, Beth felt her temper flare; she was upset after her conversation with Stephen and in no mood to be upbraided by Alex for something she had not done.

"It's nothing to do with you what goes on between Stephen and myself." She knew the words sounded bad and misleading, but she had resented his accusation and let it show in her voice. "In any case, who are you to talk, calling Cressida a young kid one minute and making love to her the next?"

His voice was like steel. "And who told you I made love to Cressida?"

"Cressida did."

"The little fool," he hissed and gave Beth no clue to his real feeling for the girl.

"Whatever I think about Cressida," he said caustically, "at least she is not married with a child. I would not have believed that you could be so two-faced, Beth Carrington."

His remark finally broke Beth's tenuous hold on her usual good temper. She struggled out of his grasp, lifted an arm and before she had thought of any action at all, had hit Alex across the mouth.

"How dare you speak to me like that when you know nothing . . . "

But words were taken from her by his mouth on hers, she was pulled tightly against him and his kiss was savage. She struggled and tried to pull away, but his insistency wore her down, and as she gave a half-sob, his lips softened on hers until in their seeking and their tenderness, they received the answer from her that he was demanding.

He let her go suddenly. "If you are going to be so free with your kisses," he jibed at her, "you can save them for me."

Tension returned to her and she tore herself from his arms and started to run from the room. "You're a beast, Alex Tomlin, it's not even worth trying to tell you the truth, and I never want to see you again." She was sobbing as she reached the door and knew he had not moved from the window; she hated him.

★ ★ ★

During the next few weeks, as winter turned to spring, Beth was to see Alex only once. He was coming out of the hall as she arrived for work; he gave her a curt nod and went on his way. She had not wished to meet him, but his dismissal hurt her nevertheless. She told herself that she had not forgiven him for the assumption he had made about herself and Stephen, yet something in her wished for a better relationship.

Stephen had apologized for the scene with Alex and Beth did not have the heart to blame him.

"Alex made a mistake, Stephen, we know there was nothing more to it than a friendly chat," she said.

"But Alex assumed otherwise, didn't he? I don't know why he was so upset unless he is keen on you himself."

Beth laughed. "Far from it, Stephen, I'm afraid we quarrelled. In any case he's got Cressida."

Stephen groaned. "She might catch him yes," he said. "She's been trying long enough, but I'm not sure what Alex makes of her. Sometimes he treats her like a kid sister, but other times I wonder." He turned to her. "But I'm sorry if I've caused an upset between you; do you want me to speak to him?"

Beth was horrified. "Don't you dare. If he wants to think things like that then let him. I couldn't care less." But even as she spoke, she knew she did care and tried to turn the conversation away from personal matters.

Occasionally she offered to take James out in the afternoons when she had finished work and Laura seemed grateful for this. There was no sign of Cressida, for which Beth was thankful, but she had no doubt that the young girl was making her presence felt at the farm.

Three weeks went past without her speaking a single word to Alex, and Beth began to think that she would finish her work at the hall without ever seeing him again. She did not know whether to be glad or sorry.

It was James who sparked off an unexpected meeting with Alex, which made her heart beat faster and brought the realization that she was pleased to see him and not the opposite.

It was a fine afternoon at the end of February and she was looking after James for an hour or two while Laura went to a design centre in Norwich. She had heard that day that they were looking for part-time greetings-card designers who specialized in plants and flowers, and although she had no hope of doing such work, Laura had told Beth that at least she wanted to find out about it.

It seemed a shame to keep James in on such a day, but when he asked to go to the farm, Beth hesitated. It did not necessarily mean that she would meet Alex, but she did not want to take the risk. But she could not resist the pleading look in James' eyes and they put on boots and set off for a walk. She had to smile, as it was James who took her — he knew the farm better than she did, and obeyed his Uncle Alex to the letter when it came to which fields they could walk through.

Beth enjoyed the tramp across the open fields in the spring sunshine; hedges were beginning to show green and the grass had lost its stunted winter flatness.

The last place that James insisted on visiting was the duck-pond and it was there that Alex found them. He came walking through the farmyard and Beth gave a start when she saw him; her heart gave a tell-tale thump and she knew that the emotion she felt was nothing short of pleasure at seeing this smiling handsome man walking towards them. There was certainly no hint of anger about him.

"James, Beth," he called.

"Uncle Alex, we've been exploring, it's more interesting than going for a walk. And we found some primroses, and lambs'-tails, Beth says they are hazel catkins, and look there's some pussy-willow over the pond. They're willow catkins, you know."

Alex gave a chuckle and ruffled James' hair. "You've been having a nature lesson, I can see. Well, do you like the ducks and would you like us to take you to see some more birds?"

The child looked up at his uncle. "Do you mean you and Beth, or you and Cressy?"

Beth's eyes met those of Alex and she saw a grin.

"Given away again," he laughed. He certainly is in a good mood, thought Beth, he has forgotten more easily than I have, I must take my lead from him.

"Shall we take the young rascal, Beth? We said we would, you know."

She looked at him almost shyly. "Yes, I would like to go, Alex."

"Good," he said. "Let's make it tomorrow then, while this good weather lasts."

They started to walk back to the house, making their arrangements as they went along. Just as they were saying goodbye and Alex called out "See you tomorrow", they were interrupted by the somewhat frosty voice of Cressida and saw her walking towards them from the kitchen door,

"Is there something on tomorrow, then?" she asked.

Beth looked at Alex; how would he handle Cressida? Then she sighed, she might have known that he would use charm.

He put his arm around Cressida and drew her towards them all, "Cressida, Beth and I are taking James to Minsmere. I didn't ask you because I know how you hate cold and wind and are bored with anything to do with the great outdoors. You curl up with a fashion book for the afternoon and we'll all have tea together when we return."

Beth had a hard job to stop herself from smiling, she might have guessed how smooth Alex could be when he chose, she discovered something new about him every time they met. But the way he had handled Cressida was nothing short of hilarious and she watched the expression changing in the girl's face.

"I don't see why you have to take Beth," she said and shot an air of hostility towards Beth who was holding on to James' hand, "but I expect she will take care of James. He never behaves when I have him, so she's welcome. I'll see you afterwards, darling," she said to Alex, and with Cressida hanging on to his arm the two of them walked back to the farmhouse, while Beth watched with amusement and then took James back to Haversham Hall.

The trip to Minsmere with James was one of those days that Beth would always remember. They didn't go into the Reserve, but parked the Range Rover on Dunwich Cliff as they had done that other night and they walked together along the shore.

It was an unusual day for East Anglia; it was still. There were not many days, thought Beth when you could be on the coast and not feel the east wind from Russia coming off the sea. There was warmth in the pale sun, and the greyness of the pebbles on the beach was almost bright in the clear atmosphere. James was excited but well-behaved at the same time — he seemed to realize that this was something of a special treat.

Beth and Alex each held on to one of his hands along the broad walk at the side of the Reserve, and she had the uncanny feeling that they could have been a happy family on an outing. Yet the tragedy was that James was here only because of the unhappiness in his own family.

It all looked so different in the daylight, mused Beth; interesting, invigorating but some of the magic had gone. Once in the hide, they watched a marsh harrier in the trees, and they laughed together as James tried to look through the binoculars but said it was all blurred. Alex promised to buy him some of his own when he was older and the little boy stayed quiet as they watched; he sensed that they were waiting for something to appear and he had his reward when a group of avocets came through the shallow water just in front of the hide. Beth pointed out their long legs and curved bill and James listened intelligently. He will try to draw them when he gets home, she thought.

There was no one about on a February afternoon in mid-week, and they had their picnic in the hide. Yet another side of Alex was revealed to Beth; he was jolly, merry . . . she couldn't find a word that didn't sound old-fashioned, and amiable sounded too formal.

He looked at her as they drank their coffee from the flask.

"I'm glad we came, Beth," he said. "I didn't like being on bad terms with you."

"I'd rather forget it, Alex, put it in the past."

"Will you let me apologize for my behaviour that day, Beth?" He was looking at her intently. "I'm sorry I misjudged you; Stephen avoided me for weeks, then a couple of days ago he suddenly came out with it — what a help you had been to him, how you had offered to have James so that he could go away with Laura. And I jumped to the wrong conclusions; I can only say I'm sorry, Beth."

He took her hand and she felt the promise, the tingle of his touch; she had that feeling that she wanted to hold on to him for ever.

"Thank you, Alex, I can understand. But it's a lovely day today and I don't want to spoil it with past quarrels."

"We must do it again," he replied. "James has obviously enjoyed it, he has been as good as gold. Do you think he is old enough for castles? We could take him to Framlingham, couldn't we?"

She was silent and watched James as he looked out of the shutter at the other end of the hide.

"You are quiet, Beth, what is the matter?"

"I'm sorry, we shouldn't be talking about him in his presence but I don't think he can hear. It's just that I feel sad that it's you and I who are taking him out, enjoying his discovery of the world. It should be Stephen and Laura, shouldn't it?"

He nodded and looked at her. "Things are no better, then?"

"Sometimes I think it will be all right, then Laura gets an idea into her head and it sparks off a quarrel. And yet I can see how she feels; she went to enquire about a job in a Norwich design centre yesterday, but she knows that Stephen won't let her go and leave James. It seems to be deadlock."

"And what would you do, Beth, if it was your child?" His tone was quiet and gentle and interested too.

Beth frowned. "It's so difficult, I am

not in the same situation as Laura; she is so frustrated. I feel myself that I would want to be with my child, and yet I don't think that James would come to any harm with a nanny, especially if his parents were happier. I know we've said all this before, but they do worry me, the two of them."

"And you won't be at Haversham much longer, Beth?"

She shot a glance at him, was there any meaning behind his question?

"No, I open the shop at Easter," she replied.

"And you will be glad?"

"I have to be honest, I love the shop and will be very happy when it opens again, but I have really enjoyed this winter at Haversham Hall; it's been an experience I wouldn't have missed for the world."

Alex was still holding her hand and lifted it and pressed a kiss into her palm; she felt a shiver go through her and looked into his eyes, but as she met his searching look, a new world seemed to open up to Beth. There was an expression in Alex's eyes she had never seen in any man's and she felt herself drowning; she knew she was thinking of love, but surely Alex did not feel love for her; and this emotion was so new and startling to her that she had no way of knowing whether it was love or just a strong attraction to the Alex she had come to know and like.

He leaned forward and put his cheek to hers, it was a warm and thoughtful gesture. She almost turned her head to seek his lips, she had a sudden wild feeling that she wanted the passionate contact, but she remembered James and stayed still, listening to what Alex was saying.

"You have come into my life, Beth, and I'm not sure what it means. Will I see you again when you leave Haversham?"

Beth did not know the answer, the spell was broken and she was forthright. "It is unlikely, we are fifteen miles apart and you have Cressida in any case."

A frown came into his face. "And you have Dave," he said.

Beth did not speak; she did not know why, it would have been easy enough to tell him about Dave. But if he was tied up with Cressida, and he had not denied it, why should she let him think that she was free?

Her emotions were complicated and she did not want complications on that pleasant day. James was beginning to run up and down the hide and she thought it was time to be off.

"Let's walk back along the sea's edge," she suggested. "I'd love to do that. And it's quiet and gentle today."

"Come on, then," Alex said. "I'll carry the picnic and you hold on to James."

The little boy loved the sea; he ran away every time a wave came in, then suddenly waded in and got his feet wet. He did not seem to mind, but Beth did.

"Oh, James, we must run back to the car and take off your wet shoes," she scolded him.

"I can walk in the sea, now," he announced. "It won't matter now I've got my feet wet."

"No, you don't," she said. Alex was walking ahead.

Some imp of mischief suddenly took hold of James and he pulled away from Beth's hand and ran into the sea; she gave a scream and ran into the icy water after him. Alex was running towards them, but before he could get there, Beth found herself in deep water where the beach shelved suddenly, clinging on to a now struggling James.

"Hold on to me, James," she yelled, as the little boy tried to find his feet in the swirling waters.

By the time Alex had reached them, she had managed to drag James out and he was a crying and bedraggled sight on the shore. Alex caught hold of her and pulled her free of the water. She clung to him, glad of the feel of his strong arms around her and his face close to hers.

"I'm sorry, Alex, one moment he was holding on to me and the next he had broken free and was in the water." She started to cry, partly with shock and partly with vexation.

"I thought I could have trusted you with him," said Alex sharply. "Hold this rucksack and I'll carry James back. We must get him into the car as quickly as we can. For heaven's sake, stop crying, James, you are only wet, you haven't hurt yourself."

They arrived at the car panting and Alex put the heater on. It took a minute or two to warm up, but Beth took off James' wet things and wrapped him in a rug which Alex kept in the back.

"Are you all right, Beth?" Alex's arm came round her. "I'm sorry I was cross, it gave you a shock didn't it? But no harm's done; we'll soon have James home. Are you very wet?"

"Only my feet and trousers," she

said. "I'll take my socks and shoes off and dry my feet on James' rug; I can turn my trousers up a bit."

"You can take them off if you like," grinned Alex.

"Alex Tomlin," Beth was furious with him. "How can you make a joke of it? You didn't see James disappear under the wave."

Alex started up the engine for reply, then before they drove off, he leaned over and gave her a quick kiss. "You are lovely," he said. "And you didn't panic, you had him out in seconds, before I could reach you. Thank you, Beth."

She smiled at him; she always liked the feel of his lips on hers and she could not be cross with him for very long.

James fell asleep on the way home and was very warm in the rug. They couldn't find Laura, so they got his pyjamas on and put him to bed.

"I'll sit with him," said Alex. "You go and have a shower and find some trousers of Laura's to put on. You are about the same size, I should think."

But Beth had suddenly thought of something.

"But, Alex, you can't stay; you promised Cressida that you would have tea with her," she said.

"Be damned to Cressida," was his explosive reply.

"You and James are more important than two Cressidas put together. I will see her tonight."

When Beth was warm and dry, she went and got Mrs Pierce to make a tray of tea for them and she and Alex sat with the sleeping James.

"You've given me a lot to think about today, young Beth," Alex suddenly said.

"What do you mean, Alex?" she asked.

"I'm not even sure myself, but it's something important and maybe I'll tell you about it one day."

He went at that, and Beth waited for Laura to return, thinking about what he had said and of how very much she could like him on these occasions.

Laura came in looking downcast. Beth told her about James but she hardly seemed to hear the words and gave her son no more than a brief glance.

"What is it, Laura?" Beth asked.

"I'm sorry, Beth, I'm a bit down. There's a super job over at Norwich, but I daren't even mention it to Stephen, we had such a row last time I broached the subject. But this seems such a splendid opportunity and it's only mornings. It's in a greetings-card studio; I would like to do it more than anything."

Beth did not know what to say; she knew Stephen's feelings, but should she try to speak to him for Laura's sake? How could one interfere in the married life of two friends? It was an impossible situation, but she did her best when she made her reply to Laura.

"Perhaps if you could make Stephen

realize that James is nearly of an age to start nursery school, he would understand," she suggested.

But Laura didn't brighten up, just shook her head. "It's hopeless," she said. "Sometimes I think I hate him; I never thought it would be like this." She turned to Beth. "Would you say something to him for me? You usually see him on a Friday, he might take notice of you."

Beth would not promise and she left Laura and the sleeping James rather unhappily.

Beth was not going to get the chance to speak to Stephen.

The next day she got in rather late, as she had stopped to go to the bank in Orborough. As she went into the library, she looked with pleasure at the pictures she had cleaned and thought that they seemed to have taken on a new lease of life.

Looking from one to another her eye met, with sudden shock and horror, a blank space on the wall.

It was where the Constable painting always hung.

She looked wildly round in case she had made a mistake, but the blank space was there and it could only mean one thing.

The Constable painting was missing.

6

BETH'S first thought was that Lord Tomlin had been in and removed the painting for some reason. She tried not to panic and calmly and carefully looked in every place she could think of in the library; as it began to sink in that the painting was nowhere to be found, she felt sick with worry. My only hope is in Lord Tomlin, she said to herself, I shall have to pluck up courage and go and ask him.

Lord Tomlin's room was empty and she searched everywhere for him, ending up in the kitchen to see if Mrs Pierce knew of his whereabouts; she was informed that he had gone to Ipswich and would be back by lunch-time.

Without saying why she wanted him, she made her way back to his room. She thought that under the circumstances he would not mind if she searched to see if the painting was there. But still it was not to be found and she went back to the library to have another look there. Convinced by now that the painting had been stolen, a wave of panic came over her; calm and common sense deserted her and with Lord Tomlin absent, the only person she could think of was Alex.

She ran all the way to the farm and Maggie said she thought that he was round at the stables. Without waiting to catch her breath, she started running to the stable block, then hurtled into Alex as he came from that direction.

"Steady on, steady on," he said. "Whatever is the matter, Beth?"

He held her arms in a tight grip.

"Alex," she cried out, then no more words came. She burst into tears and he pulled her into his arms and held her closely to him.

"Come on," he said. "Try and tell me, it can't be as bad as all that. Is it James? If I knew what was wrong, I could try and help you."

She gulped and took a deep breath. "It's the painting," she said. "It's gone."

"Painting? What painting?"

She looked at him in amazement and his lack of understanding brought her to her senses and made her realize that he had no idea what she was talking about.

"It's the Constable painting, Alex, your father's valuable Constable. It's disappeared."

"Rubbish, pictures don't disappear; do you mean it's missing from its usual place? You've probably put it somewhere different and forgotten where."

Beth pulled herself from his arms where she had derived much comfort until he had started to speak; he wasn't showing her much sympathy, he didn't even believe her.

"It's not there, Alex, it really isn't, there's just a space on the wall where it usually hangs. Would you come and have a look, Alex? Please."

He looked down at the strained and tearful face and at last his tone changed to one of kindness. "Yes, of course I will, Beth, but I'm sure that the painting can't be far away."

But an hour later, Alex was to change his mind. He helped Beth look in every place they could think of, and together they walked around the hall checking for signs of a break-in, but there was no evidence to be found.

Lord Tomlin returned and Beth found that she was shaking as she told him what had happened; he had not taken it down for any reason and the three of them stood in the library, looking at the space where the Constable had always hung.

Beth was inclined to blame herself, but Lord Tomlin would not have it.

"No, Beth, I didn't tell you to keep the library locked, it never has been locked, perhaps that was foolish. If it's anyone's fault it's mine; I suppose such a valuable painting should have been kept in the safe, but I just didn't dream that it was necessary."

Alex looked at his father. "Do you want me to call the police in?" he asked.

But Lord Tomlin was shaking his head. "Not at the moment," he replied. "There's a bit of a mystery here as it is not well known that I have a Constable in my collection; and there's no sign of anyone breaking in, so it rather reflects on friends and family, which must make us feel a little uncomfortable."

He looked from Beth's worried face to his son's handsome one. "Leave it for a few days," he said. "That's what I want to do, though I expect I should get on to the insurers. I suppose if we tell the police they would put out a warning to all art dealers, but I don't want to go to those lengths at this stage. Wait and see what happens, and stop worrying, Beth, I don't want you to go around feeling that it's your fault."

Beth turned to thank him and Lord

Tomlin returned pensively to his own room. Alex stayed with Beth and they were talking quietly about the affair and its implications, when the door burst violently open and a wild and distraught Stephen stood there.

"Beth," he cried out in agitation. "Oh, Alex, you're here too, thank goodness."

Beth went up to him and took his arm; he was holding a piece of paper, and his hand was shaking.

"What is it, Stephen?" she asked him. "Have you had bad news?"

Stephen sat down at the table and buried his head in his hands, running his fingers through his hair in distress.

"She's gone, she's gone. I had this feeling that something was wrong and I came home early, I was too hard on her. And she's taken James." His words were almost incoherent, but he suddenly looked up at them and thrust the paper towards Beth. "Read that, read that," he muttered.

'*Stephen
I can't stand any more. I'm going away and taking James. I will look after him.*

Love Laura.'

Beth read the words again and again until they finally sank in. Then going to the table, she sat with Stephen and took his hand. Alex was frowning.

"Stephen, listen to me," she said. "Did you have a quarrel? What has sparked this off? Laura wouldn't leave you without good reason, I'm sure of it."

He lifted his head and looked at her, then took her hand in both of his. "Oh, Beth," he said brokenly. "It's all my fault. Laura was offered a job in Norwich, she wanted it. Did you know about it? She was so keen." Beth nodded and he continued. "But I said she had to wait till James was school-age, I thought that was reasonable, it's only another year. I didn't dream she'd go off like this. What shall I do?"

Alex spoke for the first time. "Stephen, have you any idea where Laura might have gone? I would be quite willing to take Beth to talk to her." But Stephen was shaking his head.

"I don't know, she has a sister in London but it's only a tiny flat. Or do you think she could have gone to her parents? They live in Torquay, it seems a long way to take James."

Alex was looking from Beth to Stephen and he said rather stiffly, "Look, I must be honest, I seem to be the onlooker. Laura hasn't gone because she suspects there is something between you and Beth, has she, Stephen?"

Beth jumped up in anger and Stephen just looked bewildered.

"How dare you suggest that again, Alex Tomlin?" she raged at him. "Nothing is further from the truth and for you to say that when Stephen is so upset is nothing short of beastly."

Stephen spoke more normally for the first time. "Don't be angry, Beth, it doesn't help. I can see how it must seem to Alex, I always seem to come to you for comfort, don't I?" He looked at Alex. "But if anything is true in all this, it's that Beth has been a very good friend to me and Laura; and most important, that I still love Laura. I always have, it's just that things seem to get between us. And now she's gone with James, I just can't believe it."

"I'm sorry, old man, it's just the way things looked," Alex apologized and put out his hand to Beth. "I always seem to be making you angry. I'm sorry, Beth."

She took his hand and knew that she must forget his words for Stephen's sake. She did so by trying to be practical.

"Stephen, why don't you go and ring Laura's sister and her parents; you can find some way of putting it so they won't be suspicious, can't you?"

Stephen got up and gave her a wan smile. "Perhaps it would be a help to be doing something. I don't even know if she has any money, I don't keep her short but she has no money of her own; I'll go and have a look and see what she's taken with her, after all how am I to know if she's gone for good or just off for a few days to think things over?"

He went out and Beth looked at Alex. "He's knocked out, isn't he?" she said. "He really couldn't see the state Laura was getting into. What can we do to help, Alex?"

"I don't know, just be here for him to talk to, I suppose." He stopped and was silent, then he spoke slowly. "Has something occurred to you, Beth?"

"Whatever do you mean?"

"Well, I was just wondering if it was a coincidence that the painting has disappeared on the same day as Laura."

"Alex!"

"Don't sound so scandalized . . . "

"But Laura wouldn't have taken the painting, I am sure that it would never have entered her head, she's not that sort of person and she respects the beauty and value of a painting." Beth felt upset at Alex's suggestion.

"I don't know, she may have needed the money," he said. "Stephen seemed to think that she might be short."

"But, Alex, it's not the kind of thing you can take anywhere and sell easily, not like a piece of silver or china."

"I know that, but perhaps Laura was desperate, she may have thought of it as a quick way of making some capital." He was thoughtful for a moment, but Beth still had a sense of annoyance that he was still thinking it possible that Laura could have stolen the painting. But Alex was asking her a question, and she listened to him seriously.

"Would she find it easy to sell, Beth?"

She shook her head. "A painting like that usually comes up for auction, or it is sold by private arrangement. It's not the kind of thing you can take into an art shop and sell over the counter. It's too valuable. I would have thought that

Laura would have known that." She was shaking her head, still distressed. "Nothing will make me believe that Laura has taken it; and Alex, Stephen doesn't know about the painting yet, we were so shocked over Laura that we didn't mention it."

"Don't say anything for the time being, I don't want him to think that we link Laura with its disappearance."

Alex got up and looked at her. "Will you be all right now, Beth? I must get back." He put his hand on her arm. "Do all you can for Stephen, I promise I won't be suspicious again, I think it must have been jealousy."

Beth laughed out loud, she could not help it. "Oh, Alex, you cannot possibly be jealous, what can you mean? It would imply that there is something between us and it isn't true. You have Cressida and . . . "

"You have Dave."

It was not what she had intended to say, but again she did not correct him. There were times when she felt a little afraid of the strength of her feelings for Alex and somehow she felt safer in letting him think that she was still tied up to Dave.

But Alex was pulling her close. "Well, Dave can let me have a kiss," he said, and touched her lips briefly and softly with his. Even that casual caress had the power to stir her, and her eyes followed him for a long time as he walked across the garden to the farm.

The rest of that week dragged by with no news of Laura and no news of the painting; Alex came in to see her from time to time but never stayed for more than a few minutes. Stephen went to the City early each morning, but came back straight after lunch, and for two days Beth stayed on in the afternoon to talk to him; he had been told about the painting and felt very unhappy about it. He was racked with guilt and Beth found it hard to keep up his spirits when she was so worried herself. On the Friday, Alex sent Beth home and took Stephen off to the farm; she went gladly, feeling tired and dispirited, but when she got home the problem wouldn't go away and she almost wished she had Dave to talk to.

She usually enjoyed Saturdays; quite often there was an auction to go to, but it was a quiet time of the year and Beth half-heartedly cleaned up the flat trying to decide what to do with herself.

An unexpected knocking at the door lifted her spirits and she hurried through the living-room feeling that she would be glad to see anyone.

Alex Tomlin was the last person she had expected to see. He didn't say a word, but stepped into the room and took her in his arms. She was too surprised to protest, but the force of his lips on hers pushed her head backwards and she began to struggle. Sensing his roughness, the movement of his lips became softer and cajoling, asking for a response from her which she found she was all too ready to give. Her body was weak against his strength and she felt her arms stretch up to reach around his neck and bring his head closer.

When at last he raised his head; she dropped hers to his chest and he stroked her hair; she was bewildered and entranced at the same time and his first words did not enlighten her.

"You're a monkey, Beth Carrington." There was a teasing note in his voice and her head shot up until she could look into his eyes to see if he was serious. She saw a wicked glint there and started to smile.

"Well, I don't know why," she answered him. "And what do you think you are doing, bursting in here and . . . " she was lost for words.

"The kiss was a payment for deceiving me," he told her.

"But I haven't deceived you." She still did not know what he was talking about. "I explained about Stephen and you apologized, we've got all that straight."

"It's not Stephen, it's Dave."

She sat down on the settee with a flop and he placed himself beside her, looking into her face.

"Now I know you're mad," she said, then she remembered and stopped speaking. She had let him think she was still going out with Dave — but how could he possibly know otherwise?

"You've remembered," he said with glee. "And I have found you out. You let me think you were going out with Dave to keep me at a distance; well, I've decided I don't want to be kept at a distance after what I've learned this morning."

"Oh, Alex, stop playing with me, what has happened to make you come barging in like this?" She was half-playful, she could not be serious with an Alex in this kind of mood.

"I had business with Randall and Williams, the Estate Agents in Orborough this morning and it was Dave who advised me. On the way out, we passed a very pretty little girl in the office; he introduced her, Polly he said her name was, and he'd like me to be the first to know that they were getting engaged at the weekend, and if I saw you, to tell you and say that they would be in touch as soon as they'd arranged a party."

"Oh, Alex," Beth was laughing. "Isn't it lovely? I knew it was coming, but they certainly haven't lost much time. I am so pleased."

"And what do you mean, madam, by letting me think that Dave was still the man in your life?"

She faltered. "I don't know . . . you assumed that he was still around and the right moment to tell you never seemed to come. I didn't think it was important in any case."

His arm went round her and he drew her gently against him, his mouth against her hair. "To tell you the truth, I didn't know myself how important it was until this morning, and I'm not even sure now; but I am sure of one thing. It's Saturday and it's lunch-time; how about going out for lunch and then having a walk somewhere? Would you like to spend the afternoon with me, Beth? Or have you had enough of the Tomlin family for one week?"

"Alex, I must be honest, I would be so pleased to be able to talk to you. I can't get Laura and the painting out of my mind; in fact, when you came I had just been wishing that I still had Dave to turn to." She looked at him happily.

"And will I do instead?" he asked her with a grin.

"Yes, please," she said, and reached up and kissed him.

"No more kissing," he teased her. "It's lunch-time, let's be off to the pub."

He drove to a village near the river and after lunch, they left the car and walked. The wind was blowing strongly across the water but it had lost its wintery iciness. The swaying reeds reflected in the ripples of the water that glittered in the sunshine. For miles they could see nothing but water and trees and sky; so much sky, thought Beth, and that special East Anglian blue that was rarely without the contrast of the white scudding clouds.

Her hand was in Alex's; she felt content, something had happened to them that day and although no words were spoken, their companionship did not seem threatened by thoughts of Cressida or Laura and Stephen. They enjoyed watching the ducks and waders on the river where it widened to such an extent that the opposite bank was way in the distance.

Not wanting to break the tranquil mood, Beth did not pose the questions she had wanted to ask him, and it was Alex who first took their minds away from themselves and their surroundings.

"I'm afraid that Stephen and Father are disagreeing as to whether to inform the police about Laura's disappearance; Father thinks she might have come to some harm, but Stephen says it's a private matter. I think he's right, what about you, Beth?"

She was solemn as she thought about it. "I don't see how you can get in the police when we know why Laura has gone, even if we don't know where," she said. "And they would have to be told about the painting too; I thought your father wanted to avoid that."

"Yes, I know. I just keep hoping that the silly girl will get in touch with us, I keep thinking of James, too, poor little kid."

Beth looked up at his serious face; he really did care, she thought, and liked him for it.

They turned and walked back into the wind, laughing as they bent their heads against its strong buffeting. Back at the car, Alex turned and touched Beth's cheek with his lips. "You've got rosy cheeks," he smiled. "I think the walk has done you good. It's done me good, too."

"Thank you, Alex, you saved my life today, I don't know what I would have done if you hadn't arrived when you did."

He left her at the flat and she spent the rest of the weekend with less of a sense of worry. All was well between her and Alex at the moment; she was happy to deny all thoughts of what Cressida might mean in his life.

When she went to the hall on Monday, Beth felt hopeful that there might have been some news, but Lord Tomlin met her with a long face saying that Stephen had gone off to work and that they had heard nothing of Laura or the painting.

At the end of the morning when she was clearing up, the phone rang and Beth expected it to be Lord Tomlin, so she was startled to hear a female voice at the end of the line.

"Is that Beth?"

She thought she recognized the voice, but when she spoke it was with a sharp question.

"Who is it?"

"It's Laura."

7

"LAURA, where are you?"

"In Felixstowe."

"Felixstowe? So you're not far away?"

"No, listen, Beth, are you on your own? I want to speak to you."

"Yes, there's no one here. But are you all right, Laura? And is James all right? We've been so worried about you."

"I'm sorry, I can't tell you about it now. I want to ask you if you would come and talk to me, Beth. There are a lot of things I want to ask you. Would you come?"

Beth had no hesitation. "Yes, of course I will. Do you want me to come this afternoon?"

"Yes, please, I'll tell you the address. Have you got a pen?"

Laura said no more except that she

would be waiting at the house for her, and could Beth try not to let anyone know about the phone-call.

Beth was both troubled and excited when she put the phone down; Laura had sounded cheerful and positive and it made Beth feel more hopeful.

As she had been about to leave the hall in any case, she had no need to speak to anyone and it was very easy to keep Laura's request.

She had a quick lunch, got out the street map of Felixstowe and found the road, wondering all the time whatever Laura was doing there. It did not take her long to reach the small seaside town in spite of the usual traffic and hold-ups on the A12.

The road she was looking for was quite near the sea front and the house was one of a terrace of tall three-storeyed Victorian villas, many of them turned into guest-houses and small hotels.

Beth felt a little nervous as she knocked at the door, but nervousness was soon banished when Laura appeared with a very excited James. He threw his arms around Beth and hugged her legs and she had to smile at him. He didn't give Laura a chance to say a word.

"Beth, have you come to take me home? I want Daddy and Uncle Alex, I want to be at home not here."

Beth met Laura's eyes across the small boy's head.

"Hello, Laura," she said.

"Hello, Beth, thank you for coming," Laura replied.

"Have you been here all the time, Laura?" asked Beth, bursting with curiosity.

"Yes, an old friend of mine lives here with her husband. They have no children, but they love James. Celia always said I could come if things got bad and she gave me the whole of the top floor." She turned to James. "Sweetheart," she said. "Run along to Aunty Celia for a minute. Beth and I are just going out to have a talk, we won't be very long."

James pulled a face but went walking off towards the kitchen; a tall girl came out, holding James' hand and was introduced as Celia. James seemed quite happy with her, especially when she offered to let him help her make some biscuits.

Laura turned to Beth. "If you don't mind, I'd rather go out, we'll take my car down to the ferry. Somehow the wind blows care away down there and it's easier to think clearly."

Felixstowe Ferry had always been a favourite place of Beth's and she made no objection. The River Deben ran into the sea there and during the week when the yachtsmen were absent it could be quiet and solitary.

They left the car by one of the pubs and started walking along the bank past the Martello Tower and the golf-course.

As they turned towards the sea, and Beth could hear the waves breaking on the shore, Laura started to speak. Beth had not said anything and had thought it best to wait and let the first words come from Laura.

"Let's sit down here," Laura said, "where we can watch the sea. It has a fascination, hasn't it?"

Beth agreed and wondered when Laura was going to get to the point.

"Beth, I'm sorry, I've brought you here and now I don't know where to start. But tell me, first of all, how is Stephen? Have you been seeing him?"

Beth nodded. "Yes, I've seen him most days and tried to talk to him. You gave him an awful shock, Laura, he took it very badly." She stopped, not knowing whether to ask the next question. "What made you decide to leave so suddenly, Laura, and stay away all that time without letting us know? Lord Tomlin wanted to go to the police but Stephen wouldn't. And now you have got in touch at last; what has made you do that?"

"It's a long story, Beth can you bear with me? A lot of it you know and it all came to a head the night after I'd been to that place in Norwich. That tipped the scales for me, I saw those people doing the work that I longed to do. You will think I'm awful, that I don't love James, but it's not true. I'm an artist Beth, I can't stop painting just because I've had a child. Can you understand?"

"I think so, Laura; so you came here?"

"Yes, Stephen and I had an awful row, the worst ever and I just felt I had to get away. Celia said I should let Stephen know where I was but I couldn't. I wanted to be alone to think things over. I've been coming out to the Ferry a lot, sometimes I bring James, he loves to watch the boats."

"And did you come to any decision, Laura?"

Laura was quiet for a very long time.

"It's strange how things work out," she said slowly. "I came here to be on my own, to think things over, and do you know the only thing I could think of? Stephen. I missed him so much, I must have just taken him for granted. I'd begun to think, possibly because it was denied to me, that the most important thing in my life was my painting. But I suddenly realized it wasn't true; it was Stephen who was important, Stephen and James."

Beth gave a sigh of relief as she listened to these words. Was it going to come all right, after all?

"People are very important to us, Laura," she said.

Laura went on speaking. "It took me so long to realize it, but all this weekend, I thought I must find out how Stephen is. Does he want me back? Is he missing us? That is why I asked you to come." She turned to Beth. "I still love him, you know, all this has made no difference. If he doesn't want me back, it will be hard to bear and yet I could understand."

Beth smiled. "He does love you Laura." And she told Laura of the little incident with Alex and about

Alex's suspicions; for the first time Laura smiled.

"Oh, Beth, you have been so kind to poor Stephen, no wonder Alex was jealous. And what about you and Alex, Beth . . . ?"

Beth interrupted, "We get on quite well," she said. "But there's nothing more. He says he is a confirmed bachelor, though I don't believe him, not as long as Cressida is around."

Laura was diverted from her own troubles for a moment. "Beth, Cressida won't do for Alex. I know she is my friend, but it would be disastrous."

"She is a very determined girl, Laura, but we are not talking about her and Alex. We have to sort you and Stephen out! Is there anything I can do to help?"

Laura looked thoughtful and then frowned slightly. "Well, there is something, but it's a lot to ask you and I don't know how I've got the nerve after all that's happened."

"Try me."

"What I would really like is for Stephen to come here for a few days so that we can have time on our own together and talk things over. But without James, I mean, as much as I love James, it's impossible to have a conversation when he is around."

"So you'd like me to have James? Of course I will." Beth had no hesitation.

"Would you really, Beth? You are a darling, how can we arrange it?"

Beth thought quickly. "Would James come back with me now, do you think? We could use Alex as a carrot."

Laura laughed and laughed, and it was a sound that was good to hear, thought Beth.

"Don't dare tell Alex you likened him to a carrot," Laura said.

Beth joined in the laughter. "Let me finish, I'll take James back to Haversham and perhaps we could stay at the farmhouse for a couple of nights, or I could have him at my flat, though that wouldn't be so much fun for him. Then when Stephen comes home, I can tell him what you have said and he can come straight over. It would mean he would have a chance of seeing James too. How about that, Laura?"

Beth received an enormous hug.

"You're a darling. I've got to try and make it work, haven't I? It's worth it for all our sakes."

"Yes, I think it is worth it, Laura, you have a lovely house, a good husband and a splendid little boy; it may be hard to work out something between you, but if you still love each other, I am sure you will find a way. You've just got to find a way, Laura, and it shouldn't be too difficult."

Laura kissed her and they got up. "What's to stop us then?" she said with a big smile. "I shall never forget how much you have helped me, Beth, thank you for coming over. Let's go and get James packed up and tell him the good news, shall we?"

On the way back to the car, Beth decided to tell Laura about the

Constable painting, and waited for her reaction.

"Stolen?" cried out Laura, with genuine disbelief. "Oh, poor Grandad Tomlin, it was very precious to him. Whoever would have done such a thing, was there a break-in?"

Beth told her what had happened.

"And have you got the police in? Have they been able to help?"

"Lord Tomlin wouldn't call them in, though Alex wanted him to. You see it all happened on the day that you left and we were so upset that I don't think that Lord Tomlin could cope with the police as well." Beth felt that she was trying not to say anything that would make Laura feel that she could have gone off with the painting; she was in no doubt that Laura's reaction to the news had been full of sincerity, and she felt that she knew once and for all that Laura could not possibly have been connected with the loss of the picture.

Fortunately, Laura had more important

things on her mind and they talked about James until they were back in Felixstowe, where Laura had no trouble in persuading James to go back with Beth to his Uncle Alex.

At Haversham Hall, Beth had a job keeping up with him as he ran to the farm, and they quickly found Alex, who lifted James high in the air, his face showing a mixture of delight and incredulity.

"Where have you come from, young one?" he asked.

Beth told him about the phone-call and the trip to Felixstowe.

Alex was very serious as he looked at her. "Thank you, Beth, I don't know what we'd do without you. The next thing is to tell Stephen; will you go and see if he has come home? Bring him over here for some tea, I'll keep James with me."

Beth hurried back to the hall and went in search of Stephen, but he was not yet home. Disappointed she went to tell Lord Tomlin the news and while she was there, Stephen arrived.

"I don't know why there is so much laughter and hilarity," he said gloomily.

"Take him into the library, Beth," his father said. "You are the best one to tell him the news."

In the library, Beth turned and went into Stephen's arms; she was glad that Alex couldn't see.

"Whatever is it, Beth? It's not Laura?"

"Yes, Stephen, it is Laura."

And she sat and told him everything, and he seized her and whirled her round and ended up by kissing her.

"Beth, I mustn't get it wrong, this time. What am I to say to Laura?"

"I can't tell you that, Stephen, but I think the important thing is that she wants to talk to you." She stopped and looked at his face, so changed already from the dark-visaged look of the last weeks.

"I must not interfere, but I would like to say just one thing, Stephen. Try and remember how important her painting is to Laura; I am sure that you and James come first in her life, but painting is part of her; it is her gift, her talent and it's hard to give it up completely. She cannot do without it, you know."

He kissed her again for those words. "I won't forget. And now I must go and see James, though I'm not sure that it wasn't his Uncle Alex that he wanted to see most."

But Stephen was soon proved wrong. He received a rapturous greeting from James and for the next half-hour, the little boy did not let go of Stephen's hand.

Stephen went to pack an overnight bag and Alex and Beth saw him off. As the car disappeared down the drive, Beth found that she had tears in her eyes. "Oh, Alex," she said, turning to him. "Do you think it's going to be all right?"

"I do," he replied. "I feel sure that they will sort out something sensible. They still love each other, don't they?"

"Yes, that is the most important thing." She looked down at James. "And what are we going to do with James?" She smiled at him. "Would you like to stay at the farm with Uncle Alex or come to my flat with me?"

"Uncle Alex," said James, decidedly.

"That's put me in my place," Beth said. "Very well, I'll be on my way home."

But Alex had something further to say. "Beth, I've thought of something that would be nice. Why don't you come and stay at the farm until Laura and Stephen get back? I'll get Maggie to stay for a couple of nights, she won't mind, in fact she'll be glad to have you."

Beth could not help sounding pleased. "I think I would like to, thank you, Alex. I'll just go and tell your father and then I'll pop home and get my stuff and a change of clothes."

Later that evening, just as the light was fading and James was fast asleep in bed, Alex suggested a walk across the fields. It was a fine night, though not warm. The sun had gone down and the trees and hedges were dim shapes in the gathering dusk.

Beth told Alex what had happened that afternoon and he seemed encouraged to think that Stephen and Laura would find a solution to their problems.

"I think they've both had their eyes opened by all this," said Beth. "If they don't understand and sort out their problems now, I don't think they ever will, but I am hopeful."

Alex looked at her serious face and his arm came round her shoulders as they walked across the uneven grass of the field. "We'd better get back before it gets too dark and cold. I think I like having you under my roof Beth. It seems proper."

"It is most improper," she laughed jokingly. "But we have Maggie as a chaperone."

"You haven't many more days with us, have you, Beth?"

"The end of next week," she said. "I shall be sorry to leave you all."

"It's not going to be the end though, Beth, is it?"

"What do you mean?"

"This," he said and turning her towards him, took her in his arms and kissed her. The soft insistent pressure made a fiery feeling run right through her. He had the power to do this to her, the power to make her want to give back more than just a kiss.

"It's not the first time I've kissed you," he said lightly, giving her time to catch her breath. "And I don't want it to be the last. I'm just getting to know you, Beth, and I want this to be a beginning, not an end."

Beth had no reply, she was too deeply stirred, and they walked slowly on, neither of them speaking. Alex obviously did not wish to say anything further and Beth somehow felt a great happiness that he was talking about a beginning.

As they came to the gate into the

farm-yard, a sharp voice called across from the house.

"Alex, is that you? Where have you been? I thought I should see you tonight."

Beth felt Alex stiffen at her side and she knew that it was Cressida.

"Damn," she heard him mutter.

As they came into the light of the lamp at the back door, Cressida walked towards them; she was wearing boots as she often did and they seemed to give her greater height and grace.

But her voice had nothing graceful in it. "But you have someone with you. It's never . . . it's Beth. What on earth are you doing out there in the dark?"

The caustic question somehow amused Beth even though it had broken into the reverie of Alex's last words; but Alex was not amused.

He took Cressida's arm to guide her back into the house. "It's nothing to do with you, Cressida. Beth happens to be staying the night here and we went for a stroll after dinner."

Beth heard the indrawn hiss from the other girl and she wondered if Alex had deliberately provoked her with his words.

"Beth is staying? What does that mean? Are you telling me the truth?"

Beth could sense that Alex was getting angry at all the questioning, but he seemed to be trying hard not to lose his patience with Cressida.

"It so happens, Cressida, that we have James back and Beth is staying for a couple of days to look after him."

He had succeeded in diverting Cressida's attention.

"Yes," he said to her. "If you will stop concerning yourself about the state of affairs between myself and Beth, we will go and make some coffee and tell you all about it."

Cressida leaned across and kissed Alex on the cheek and he smiled at her. "That's better," he said. "I want no hard words between us."

They were a strange trio, Beth thought, as she sat looking at Alex and Cressida. Here am I feeling slightly put out because Cressida has commandeered Alex's attention and yet it seems it is her place to do so. And here is Cressida jealous because she found me with Alex. She looked at Alex and the charm of his face as he talked to Cressida; Laura had been horrified at the thought of Alex and Cressida together, but they made a striking couple and seemed to have an easy relationship. Beth was thoughtful; perhaps life won't be quite so complicated once Stephen and Laura return, she said to herself, and I can settle down and open up the shop again.

8

STEPHEN and Laura came back two days later. Beth had worked as usual in the morning and then looked after James in the afternoon to give Maggie a break. Things between Alex and herself continued in a friendly way, but since their meeting with Cressida he had made no more enigmatic remarks alluding to the future.

They were all sitting in the farmhouse kitchen having tea, when Stephen and Laura appeared and there was general commotion and excitement. James, for all his young years, seemed aware of the happy smiles of his parents and couldn't stop hugging them and telling them about his days with Uncle Alex.

Beth looked at the two of them and marvelled. They looked as though they had just come back from a honeymoon, she thought, so happy together and so pleased to be a united family again.

She caught Laura's eye and the two of them slipped upstairs to Beth's room. They sat on the bed and Laura could hardly stop talking.

"Beth, I shall never be able to thank you. It was the right thing to do, just a couple of days on our own and Stephen has been wonderful."

She told Beth of their plans for the future and Beth thought that Stephen had worked nothing short of a miracle.

Once it was established that Laura had no knowledge of the missing Constable, it did not take Alex long to persuade his father to call in the police. It started a rather unpleasant time for them all, and although Beth knew that Lord Tomlin had done the right thing, she had many moments of unease and regret. What started as a routine investigation, brought immediate trouble to the family from a completely unexpected quarter.

Detective Sergeant Quarrie, a young

man in plain clothes, was not only good-looking, he was polite, insistent and very thorough. He talked to Lord Tomlin for almost the whole morning before he was even taken into the library; by that time, Beth was shaky and nervous, dreading the interview that was to come.

Lord Tomlin smiled at her as he made the introductions. "Don't look so scared, Elizabeth. I have put Sergeant Quarrie into the picture as far as the family is concerned, and we will have to get hold of Cressida as I have had to tell him that she is like one of the family and has the run of the house. Then there will be fingerprints and the inspection to see if there was a break-in, though we know that seems unlikely." He lost his smile. "I am afraid I am in trouble for not insisting that at least we kept the library locked when it held such a valuable painting; you are not to be blamed for that, my dear, so stop worrying. I will leave you to Sergeant Quarrie now."

Sergeant Quarrie might have looked pleasant enough, thought Beth as the interview proceeded, but he makes me feel as though I'm the prime suspect. Most of his questions were about her business in Orborough and about her contacts in the art world. She was amazed at his knowledge of local art personalities and could only assume that in the CID there were specialists for every field of crime.

Alex came over after that, and he was still with the sergeant, when Lord Tomlin appeared accompanied by an older gentleman whom Beth had never seen before. He was tall and thin with grey hair and had a very worried look about him.

Beth sat quietly in the corner of the library and listened to the conversation with some surprise and many misgivings.

"Sergeant Quarrie," said Lord Tomlin, "I am sorry to interrupt, but there is an unexpected development. May I introduce Mr Samuel Blake, he is my near neighbour, a very old friend and the father of Cressida whom you have been trying to contact."

"Mr Blake," the sergeant said politely. "I think I spoke to you on the phone, have you asked your daughter to come and see me? She needn't be worried, it is only a matter of routine."

Samuel Blake's expression was troubled but he spoke calmly, "I am very sorry, Detective Sergeant Quarrie, but I am afraid that my daughter has gone away rather suddenly. I gave her your message, thought she was on her way to Haversham Hall this morning, but after lunch I noticed her car was missing; then I found a note to say that she had gone up to Edinburgh for a few days to stay with an old friend of hers. I know that she did have a friend from Scotland from her schooldays but I had no idea she had kept in touch with the girl. I must confess to feeling rather baffled by it all."

There was a still silence in the room as he finished speaking; Lord Tomlin was frowning; Beth's eyes met Alex's questioning ones, and Sergeant Quarrie was the first to speak.

"It's quite all right, Mr Blake, I understand, perhaps you would be good enough to keep in touch with me for the next few days in case you have news of your daughter." He looked round at them all and smiled briefly. "I think I have done all I can do for the time being, except that I will see your housekeeper, Mrs Pierce, I think you said her name was, on my way out; I will come back this evening to see Mr and Mrs Stephen Tomlin. We will do all we can to recover your painting, Lord Tomlin, and tomorrow I will send colleagues over for inspection and fingerprints."

He politely said goodbye, and Lord Tomlin and Mr Blake followed him out of the library.

Beth dared not look at Alex, her thoughts were racing fast and furious, and she knew that they were not charitable.

But Alex came over to her and spoke her name in rather a strained manner. "Beth, what are you thinking?"

She raised her eyes to his and she saw a worried look there. "I'm sorry Alex, I know I shouldn't be thinking this, but why has Cressida taken off for Scotland the minute she knew she was wanted by the police?"

"I think there is probably a perfectly good reason," replied Alex, with false cheerfulness. "She is an impulsive girl. I hope you are not thinking that Cressida had anything to do with the theft of the picture; I know Cressida, she may he a difficult girl in some ways, but she would never have done anything like that. I am sure of it."

Beth wasn't so sure of it, but she dare not say any more; she would have to believe Alex.

"I'm going home now, Alex, I don't feel I can work any more," she said in a tired way.

"Try not to worry, Beth. We will see you tomorrow." He said no more and seemed lost in his own thoughts, so Beth gathered her things together, left the hall and went quickly home.

The next morning, she felt a reluctance to go into work and was surprised when the telephone rang about half-an-hour before she was due to leave.

"Detective Sergeant Quarrie, Miss Carrington."

Beth gave a gasp and just managed to say, "Good-morning."

"I think it will be necessary for us to have a look at your shop and the studio. Can you arrange to be there by nine o'clock? Thank you very much."

He rang off before Beth had time to say a word or to recover from his abrupt manner.

She sat down trembling, the phone still in her hand.

What did it mean?

They suspected her of having the painting in the shop?

She could not believe it and she made herself some strong coffee to try to quieten her nerves.

She walked round to the shop hoping that the action would steady her, but when she saw the sergeant's car already outside, and the tall dark grey-suited figure standing at the door, she felt a shiver of apprehension go through her.

Afterwards Beth thought that it was the most miserably tense morning she had ever spent in her life. She was bewildered by the questions, upset because so many pictures had to be moved about, and totally at a loss when Detective Sergeant Quarrie insisted on turning out the whole of the studio. He showed her nothing but politeness, but underneath she could sense the inner core of steel, and every time she gave him an answer she could not help wondering if she was further implicating herself.

She was exhausted when he left her and just sat immobile at her table in the studio; then she remembered Lord Tomlin and rang his number.

"Elizabeth, where are you? Are you all right?"

"I'm at the shop, Lord Tomlin." Then words seem to slip from her without her giving them any thought. "I've had the detective sergeant here all the morning, and I'm sorry, Lord Tomlin, that I'm going to let you down, but I know I'm under suspicion of stealing the Constable painting, and I'm not going to come back to the hall any more . . . I didn't take it, you know . . . " Beth put the receiver down, too upset to say anything else and she did not wait to hear what he had to say. The phone rang immediately, but knowing it would be him she did not answer it. Without thinking of what to do next she automatically set about putting the studio to rights, a leaden sick feeling in her stomach that she could not dispel. She was lost in troubled thoughts and speculation, when she heard a violent rattling and banging at the shop door.

Startled, she looked out of the studio and saw that of all people it was Alex.

She opened the door to him and promptly burst into tears. He guided through back into the studio, shut the door, then held her tight against him.

"My darling girl, what has happened? Please don't cry like that."

The whole of the events of the last twenty-four hours flooded over into Beth's tears, and she sobbed into Alex's jacket, clinging to him and thankful for his strong arms about her.

"I'm sorry, Alex," she whispered.

"Sit down and tell me all about it. Father said you have had the police here, I came straight away. He is very worried."

She told him then, holding his hand and looking into kind eyes which she had so often seen cold and angry. She tried to assure him that she had not taken the painting even if it looked as though she had. She realized that she must be the obvious suspect, she said, with all her picture contacts for selling it, but she would never have taken it, never.

"Beth, stop, please stop," he said, trying to speak firmly and convincingly. "We don't believe you stole it for a moment. You must believe that; you must believe that to the police this is just a routine. They don't leave a stone unturned. We've had them at the hall all the morning, I'm glad you weren't there, though neither Father nor I dreamed that they would be here too. I think Father is regretting that he ever called them in." He had been holding on to her hand all the time, and he lifted it to his lips and smiled at her. "You are going to do what you are told now; did you walk round here? Good, you can come in my car and I will bring you back tonight; we'll go straight off to the farm and Maggie will get us some lunch. I would take you to the pub but I know you won't feel like going out. Then this afternoon, you can have a chat with Father and tell him what has happened."

Beth spoke at last.

"I don't know how to thank you,

Alex, I will do what you say. You have made me see things in perspective." She suddenly thought of something. "Alex, has there been any news of Cressida?"

"No, not a word, we seem to have landed ourselves into a pile of trouble, don't we? But come along, and we will talk about something else, Laura is worried about you too, and will be pleased to see you."

Beth calmed down after a pleasant lunch with a kind and considerate Alex and then a long chat with Lord Tomlin and Laura. She did some work and by the end of the afternoon, things seemed to be returning to normal.

Two days went by with no further contact with the police except a message from Sergeant Quarrie to say that all dealers and galleries had been alerted, and Lord Tomlin would have to be prepared to wait. Anxiety over Cressida was allayed when her father received a postcard from Edinburgh to say that she was having a nice time and wasn't sure when she would be back.

Beth was working quietly the next day when she was disturbed by the door being opened fiercely and Alex coming into the library with Lord Tomlin at his heels.

She took one look at Alex's face and jumped up in alarm; she had never seen him so agitated.

"Alex, what is it?"

"Beth, I have to tell you quickly. I'm on my way up to Edinburgh and I'm taking Father with me. We've had a phone-call from the police there, they are holding Cressida; she was caught trying to sell the Constable painting in an art shop this morning."

She looked at him in horror, unable to believe what he was saying, forgetting her first thoughts when Cressida had fled.

"Oh, Alex, and Lord Tomlin, I am sorry. She must have had it all the time, but . . . "

Alex gripped her arm. "Don't say

any more, Beth, Cressida is going to need all our help, poor little girl." His voice had softened and Beth could hear the note of affection in it as he spoke. "We will set off straight away and call and see Mr Blake as we go, he is going to be very upset. We'll just have to hope that all goes well and that we can bring Cressida and the painting back with us tomorrow."

They went out and Beth sat dumbfounded. I'll go and find Laura, she thought, I've just got to speak to someone.

Laura was busy painting, James being engrossed in a jigsaw, and she was pleased to see Beth.

"Is there any news?" she asked.

Beth told her about Cressida and Laura did not interrupt, they were both silent, their thoughts taken up with the unhappy young girl.

"What a silly, silly girl," said Laura. "But, Beth, if she had got away with selling the picture, how do you suppose she would have explained to any of us just how she was suddenly the possessor of a large fortune? I presume she wanted the money to get her to model school, I know she was desperate but I would never have believed that she would have gone to such lengths."

"It's hard to understand her at all," Beth replied. "I'm afraid it's quite beyond me how anyone could steal a painting, especially from someone like Lord Tomlin. He has always been so kind to her."

"I don't suppose we shall ever know the full story; Alex will have the job of sorting her out. I think he is the only one to have any influence over her." Laura looked at Beth. "I expect he was upset."

Beth nodded. "Yes, I have never seen him so rattled, I think it has really shaken him. But I'd better get back to the library, Laura, I've only a short time left, you know, and want to finish if I can. Thank you for talking to me, we'll just have to have patience until they get back."

The Tomlins and Cressida returned late the next morning and Lord Tomlin came into the library carrying the missing Constable.

Beth started to her feet and gave an exclamation.

"Oh, Lord Tomlin, you've brought it back . . ." she faltered. "And Cressida?"

"Alex has taken her home. It's a long sad story, Beth, but fortunately the police were very understanding once they knew I did not want to press charges, and Cressida was able to come home with us. She is shaken by her experience and full of remorse but Alex will keep an eye on her. She has been a very silly girl and I shall have to see what I can do for her. I am glad to have the picture back, it will be nice to see it in its proper place again, but of course it will have to be kept locked up now. I must go, my dear, I have Detective Sergeant Quarrie coming to see me. He will want to be satisfied that they can close the case, they have been very efficient."

Beth looked at him with a question in her eyes. "How did it come about that they caught Cressida at all?" she asked.

"We have a sharp art dealer to thank," replied Lord Tomlin. "She went into his shop to sell the picture; he took one look at it, thought he recognized it from the police description he had received only the day before, pretended an interest in it and told her he would go and get his catalogue. Cressida wasn't suspicious, and while he was in his office, he phoned the police, then kept Cressida talking until they arrived. I'm afraid she had an awful shock and was taken to the police station for questioning; but perhaps she deserved it, Beth. Do you think I am being hard?"

"No, far from it, I know you will show her every kindness in spite of the trouble she has caused. It's a good job she has Alex, isn't it?"

"Yes, it's a good job she has Alex," he repeated and, looking at her searchingly, went out and left her with her own thoughts of Alex and Cressida.

9

WITH less than two weeks to go before her work on the pictures was due to finish, Beth was kept very busy indeed, and during that time she did not see Alex; neither did she have any news of Cressida and she had no idea how the girl had faced up to her ordeal.

A happy Laura with a mischievous James popped in most days, but she did not stay long. In Beth's last week, she was invited to dinner with them in the evening after Stephen had come home and was delighted to see them and hear about the changes in their lives and their relationship.

Stephen had agreed to get someone to look after James so that Laura could open up a studio of her own in some of the many spare rooms of the hall. Workmen and painters were already busy and Laura had been interviewing young people who were interested and had enough talent to join the project of designing greetings-cards.

Beth reached the day before she was to finish at the hall without having seen Alex and was feeling a sense of disappointment. He must he seeing a lot of Cressida, she thought, and had a feeling of hopelessness, not only for herself but for Alex as well.

That morning, she let herself into the library knowing that she had little left to do and was surprised to be greeted by a male voice.

"Is that you, Beth?"

Alex was standing by the French window.

"Alex," she said, as she went up to him. "It's so nice to see you, did you know that tomorrow is my last day?"

"Yes, I did, and I'm sorry that I have not seen you. I've been away in Wales at a conference and I only got back last night. As it's your last day, I wondered if you would like a day out."

"You mean today?" she asked.

"Yes, why not? It's not nine o'clock yet, we've got a whole day in front of us."

Beth flushed with pleasure. "I'll just go and see your father," she said.

Beth went through to tell Lord Tomlin what they proposed to do and there was a look in his eye that seemed to give approval to the trip.

As they started off down the lanes, Beth said, "Where are we going?"

"Cambridge," returned Alex. "I've a fancy to take you there. It's ages since I've been there except on business."

In Cambridge, the students had gone and the Easter visitors not yet arrived, so they had a rare glimpse of the city when it wasn't quite so crowded. They left the car near Midsummer Common and walked down past Jesus College into the town.

Beth had her hand in Alex's and gradually the charm of the city overtook her. At King's College, Alex insisted that they had a look in the chapel before walking down to the river. There was a buzz of tourists here, but the organ was being played and Alex led her to a quiet place, and they sat down, still holding hands. He did not say anything and Beth was content to stay quiet and listen to the music as she glanced round at the lofty arches and the beautiful vaulting.

She felt peaceful and knew that the feeling did not all emanate from the building; the man so close to her was in a strangely quiet mood and Beth sensed that they were sharing an experience of some mystery and beauty in one of the loveliest settings in England.

As the music came to a close, Alex got up and with his arm round her, led her into the bright light of open green outside the chapel.

"Thank you, Beth," he said.

She glanced up at him with a query in her eyes, and he surprised her with a grin.

"Thank you for not telling me about the price of the jewellery you are going to wear with your new dress when we go out to dinner."

"Cressida!" she exploded; he had broken a spell, but it had been so deeply spiritual that perhaps it had needed to be broken.

"Oh, Beth, I shouldn't have said that, but I couldn't help remembering. I brought her here once and she didn't stop chattering the whole time. How anyone can look so beautiful and be so dim-witted is impossible to understand." He was smiling at her now, the serious mood had passed as they walked towards the River Cam.

"She is very young, Alex, and she seems to have only two thoughts in life. They are you and her modelling career," Beth chuckled. "I suppose I am being catty now."

"Not you, Beth, it's not in you. It's the truth and I suppose I must take the responsibility."

"How is she, Alex?" said Beth tentatively.

Alex had no hesitation. "She was ashamed of herself for about one day, she just didn't seem to realize what she had done."

It seemed to be all he wanted to say about Cressida and it left Beth thinking about his remark on his responsibility for the girl. Did it mean he meant to marry Cressida in spite of what he had always said, not only about Cressida but about marriage in general and remaining a bachelor?

There are a lot of confusing emotions about today, she thought; I felt as though I could have loved Alex when we were in the chapel, just for a short while, and I almost felt as though he was thinking the same, but it must have been my imagination because of our surroundings. But I must not let my feelings spoil the day, she said to herself, and slipped her hand into his and was glad of the answering pressure and the smile he gave her.

"Shall we have a boat, Beth? It's the thing to do in Cambridge, you know, no visit is complete without a trip on the river."

She looked to see if he was joking, but he was already making for the place where the boats were tied up, taking her assent for granted.

Beth enjoyed that hour, it was light-hearted and showed her an Alex in his most outgoing and youthful mood. They had many laughs at the near misses with other boats, and as they got further from the bridge and glided along the cool, smooth water, the atmosphere between them was soothing and harmonious.

Alex took hold of her hand to help her on to the bank and smiled down at her, almost echoing her thoughts. "I enjoyed that," he said. "It made me feel young again."

"Oh, Alex," she laughed. "As though you are old, you don't seem much older than me!"

He dropped a kiss on her cheek. "I can give you five years, young lady," he said. "And it doesn't matter what my age is, the most important thing to me at the moment is food. What do you say to us buying some food and bringing it down under the trees by the river? It seems too nice a day to stay indoors."

He was right; although they were not quite into April, the sun was warm and there were even one or two summer dresses to be seen. So they went to the nearest shop and bought sandwiches and fruit and, to Beth's amusement, cans of Coke.

Alex seemed reluctant to leave to start the journey back to Suffolk and stretched out lazily among the trees. The whole scene was conducive to relaxation; the walls of the old college buildings graced the scene in whichever direction one looked, giving an air of easy tolerance to the world rushing heedlessly by. Beth did not mind, she was in Alex's hands this day which was becoming more entrancing with every minute that passed.

She was very conscious that there was

only one more day to go at Haversham and turned to him wondering if he was thinking the same.

Almost in reply to her thoughts, he held his hand against her cheek and she leant against him. Then taking his hand away, his lips came near, brushing the soft skin. She turned her head towards him and knew she was seeking the touch of his lips on hers; her whole body felt the sensation of his nearness and the only thing in the world she wanted was to be closer to him.

But Alex was in no mood to hurry, his fingers found the soft roundness of her shoulder and drew her towards him. His mouth was on her hair, her eyes before he found her lips. The kiss was long and searching and awakened in Beth all the feelings she knew she wanted to recognize for this man. She did not worry that he did not speak to her, words did not seem to matter at that moment. And what could he have said to her that would have matched the time, the place and the mood?

When it came, his voice was playful and she was glad that he was avoiding the emotional, even though subconsciously there were words she longed to hear.

"Beth Carrington, you seem to have a power over me that I am not sure that I like. You make me think things that I don't want to think. I like to be in command of my feelings, you know."

She looked at his teasing face. "It would take a lot more than me to make you lose control over your feelings, Alex Tomlin, I am sure of that."

He touched her nose with his finger. "There is something about you I can't resist," he said. "Have you enjoyed our day out, Beth?"

"Yes, I have, thank you, it's been a nice finish to my time at Haversham Hall."

"Beth, tomorrow is not going to be the end. I'm not going to let you go out of my life when I've just discovered you, I've told you that before. Would you like to see me again once you are tucked up in your little shop?"

He took her hand as he asked the question and she was glad to return the pressure of his. "Yes, Alex, I would like it very much, if that is what you want."

"It is what I want, young lady, and it is what I am going to have."

This sounded just like Alex and Beth laughed as they got up and walked back to Midsummer Common. The drive home was quick and quiet and it was getting dark as they reached Haversham Hall.

Alex asked her to go in for coffee before she drove back to Orborough, and they went in the back door of the farmhouse and straight into the kitchen.

They heard footsteps coming from the front of the house and a high-pitched querulous voice calling Alex's name. It was Cressida.

"Alex, where on earth have you been?" Then the tone changed to one of scorn. "Oh, I might have known it, you've been with Beth."

"Cressida . . . " Alex started to say.

"I've been waiting here the whole evening. I couldn't think where you'd got to; Maggie told me you were back from Wales and I was sure you would come and see me as soon as you got back." Cressida went up to him and put her arms round his neck. "Say you're glad to see me, Alex. I've missed you. Wherever have you been to keep you out so late?"

Beth waited tensely to see how Alex would handle a peeved-sounding Cressida. Then she drew in her breath sharply as she watched Alex put his arm round the girl and give her an affectionate kiss.

"Sorry, Cressy, I didn't think we'd be as late as this. Beth and I have been to Cambridge for the day."

There was scorn in Cressida's voice again. "Not Cambridge, you took me there once, do you remember?"

Alex pulled her arms away from him. "I do," he said sharply.

But Cressida was not going to let

him off the hook. "Did you have a nice time in Wales, darling?" she asked him.

"It was hard work," he said somewhat abruptly. "And it will be even harder work now that I've got back after being away for a week."

"I'm surprised you had time to take Beth out today," said Cressida. And she dominated the conversation all the time they had their coffee, leaving Beth to get quieter and quieter and more and more angry. What was Alex playing at?

She got up to go to her car and Alex insisted on going with her, telling Cressida that he wouldn't be long.

Neither of them spoke as they walked across the garden of Haversham Hall to Beth's car.

As they reached it, Beth tried to be polite. "Thank you for taking me out today, Alex," she said. "I enjoyed it for the most part."

"Beth, you are annoyed, is it because of Cressida?" he asked.

"No," she said coolly. "I don't blame Cressida. You have obviously led her to believe that you care for her and she felt neglected."

"So you are cross with me," he said. "Don't let us spoil a lovely day by quarrelling, Beth."

"The day is spoiled," she replied. "It was spoiled when you put your arms round Cressida and kissed her. What does it mean, Alex Tomlin? Doesn't it mean anything to you at all? Is that what it is? The confirmed bachelor, as you once said, but very clever at stringing two girls along, aren't you?"

He took her arm, but she shook off his hand, she wanted no more contact with him.

"Beth, you can't be jealous, not of Cressida. I've told you before that she's just a kid to me. I'm very fond of her, she knows that and she also knows that it's no more than that."

"She doesn't know it," burst out Beth. "She is convinced that you are going to marry her, she told me so, and you don't make a very good job of letting her think otherwise. You are despicable, unless you really do mean to marry her. And you've no such intentions, have you? You just enjoy having two girls in tow for the fun of it. Well, I'm not going to be one of them," she shouted at him. "Do you hear? I loathe you and I don't care if I never see you again. In fact, now I come to think of it I probably never will see you again. So this is goodbye, Alex, are you listening? Goodbye."

"Beth . . . "

But she took no notice of him, got into the car and roared off down the drive, leaving him standing there.

Tears were streaming from her eyes and it didn't make driving easy; nor did the fact that she was in a rage. Fortunately, she knew every inch of the way and at that time of night she met very little traffic.

Such was her fury that it seemed only minutes before she was pulling up outside her flat and let herself in, flung herself on the settee and howled with anger and resentment, jealousy and bitterness; all vicious emotions which had built up into a hatred of Alex Tomlin; the fact that she had been so near to loving him earlier in the day, had enjoyed his touch, his kisses, only served to make things worse. She had believed in him, trusted him, more than liked him and it was all destroyed.

Beth tried to comfort herself with the thought that the next day was to be the last at Haversham Hall, but this only brought on a fresh fit of crying when she realized that the last day at the hall would also be the last contact with Alex Tomlin. She knew that the feeling was totally illogical, considering how angry she had been with him, but it seemed only to emphasize the complete confusion of her heart.

Next day, on her last journey to Haversham, Beth drove slowly and miserably through the lanes and hardly noticed the hedgerows in their fresh green and the trees losing their winter bareness, showing their new leaves with a burst of proud but delicate beauty.

She walked into the library and looked round; she had to admit to herself that the pictures looked lovely. My main purpose has been achieved, she thought, I ought not to feel miserable. But the remembrance of Alex and the quarrel with which they had parted plunged her into gloom again. It would have been better if I had not come in this morning, she said to herself, there is nothing more I can do.

She went to find Lord Tomlin to tell him she had finally finished; he came back into the room with her, tall and dignified, his face shining with pleasure at the sight of his paintings.

"I have been having a look at them, Beth, and you have done splendidly. I know that I should have had the paintings cleaned years ago, but I'm glad I waited for you to come along. Now, I can't let you go today without giving you a little present, and I have thought of something that might please you. I could have given you jewellery or chocolates, but I don't think you are that sort of girl."

Beth looked at him, wondering what he was going to produce; he had opened the drawer of a cabinet in which were kept his loose drawings and unframed prints; nothing valuable but all attractive and certainly worth keeping. Beth had looked at them.

He took the whole sheaf and held them out to her. "Have a look at them, Beth, I hope there might be something you can use in the shop; perhaps some of them could be framed and they will be more use to you than shut up in a drawer here."

Beth was overcome by his kindness and stammered her thanks; they looked at the prints together and were so absorbed that they did not notice that Alex had come into the room until he was standing over them.

Beth straightened up and felt herself freeze; she did not want to see Alex but he was staring at her fixedly, an enigmatic expression on his face.

"Beth," he said. "I didn't know Father would be here. I want to apologize . . . "

"I don't think I want to hear it," she said stiffly.

Lord Tomlin looked from one to another; they looked as though they were about to quarrel; the smile had gone from Beth's face, she looked downcast and her eyes were hard. He made a movement towards the door, but Alex stopped him.

"Don't go, Father, I am sure you wish to say goodbye to Beth, and I have only one thing to say to her."

Beth looked at him then and he came and stood in front of her, "I know you are thinking the worst of me, Beth, but please remember that if you ever need me, you will find me at the farm. Goodbye." With these words, he turned away from them both and stalked out of the room.

Lord Tomlin chose to take no notice

of his son, and walked with Beth to her car.

"Goodbye, Beth and thank you again. I hope you will come and see us," he said in a kindly way. "And above all, try not to read too much into Alex's concern for Cressida." And with these enigmatic words, he shook hands with her, and she drove back to Orborough.

Beth felt upset and disturbed when she got home, but that evening, she went for a walk along the shore and the wide skies and the crashing seas helped to restore her sense of calm. Just as she was discovering the person who was Alex Tomlin, she had lost him; but she tried to remind herself that she still had the shop and enough work to keep her busy and to start a new period in her life. Haversham Hall and all who lived there she must put securely into the past.

She opened the shop and had a busy Easter week, but then there was to be a lull before the next Bank Holiday;

and it was at this time that Beth could not seem to concentrate on her work, her thoughts always straying in one direction, to Alex Tomlin. And so it was she began to miss him and long to see him; to regret her hasty temper and to remember that on that last morning, he had come to apologize and she had dismissed him. I've lost him, she thought, and now that I've lost him, I want him. And it became rather a desolate feeling to find that she loved him, for the love had no hope and although she knew that on many occasions they had reached a loving togetherness, she also knew that she had lost him to Cressida.

This period, when she struggled for peace of mind, came to an abrupt end one Wednesday with a visit from Lord Tomlin.

The shop was empty and they talked pictures for a long time; Beth showed him her new stock and tried to sell him so many paintings that it caused a good deal of laughter between them.

He was glad to see her laugh, he had been dismayed by the bleak, thin look on her face when he had come into the shop.

"That's better, Beth," he said. "It is good to hear you laugh. I had begun to think that there was something very wrong, you looked so sad."

She was startled by his observation; surely her feelings didn't show on her face to that extent?

"What is it, Beth?" he said gently. "You can tell me, you know."

"You are as kind as ever, Lord Tomlin, but it's something I feel I can't discuss."

"Is it that scapegrace son of mine?" he asked.

"Alex?" She lifted her head quickly and met his twinkling eyes.

"Yes, Alex; I had a feeling that you liked him and that he liked you. You may think I'm a bit of a recluse, but I notice things, you know. And I was just beginning to feel heartened, when Cressida put her foot in it, didn't she?"

"Yes, you are right," she replied. "Alex and I had a quarrel and I haven't seen him since."

"And was Cressida the cause of the quarrel?"

"Well, yes, she was," Beth said ruefully.

"You thought that Alex was going to marry her?" He was very persistent, she thought.

"She seemed certain that he would," she said.

Lord Tomlin came and sat in front of Beth at the table in the corner of the shop.

"Beth, you may think that I'm an old fool, but I want you to listen. Cressida has been after Alex ever since she started to grow up, and I'm not saying that Alex did the right thing. He didn't take her seriously, but he made quite a lot of fuss of her. She always has been a lovely girl, you know. I watched them and I knew what was in her mind, her father did too. She had two ambitions in life, to go to model school and to marry Alex."

"She told me that, Lord Tomlin," interrupted Beth.

"Well, I must tell you that Samuel Blake is my closest friend and I've always been fond of young Cressy, but as wife to a man like Alex, I regard her as quite unsuitable. Not that it's anything to do with me who Alex chooses for his wife, but I do think that a marriage between Alex and Cressida would be nothing short of disaster. He doesn't love the girl and would only be marrying her out of pity." He was silent for a moment. "I don't know why he can't choose a nice girl like you." He was smiling at Beth and looking at her straight in the eyes.

"Lord Tomlin," cried out Beth, feeling very uncomfortable. "You can't say things like that."

"I mean it, Beth, I've become very fond of you and I believe that I've seen something in your eyes that tells me that you care for Alex. And when I arrive today, that something is missing and you are looking sad. Can you deny it?"

Beth sighed. "I will be honest with you, I do care for Alex, but it's no good match-making, Lord Tomlin. I shall never even see him again, I said some awful things to him and he will never forgive me. He is too fond of Cressida, you know."

"He may be fond of Cressida, but he will soon forget her now that she has gone to London," he said with an eye on her face.

Beth looked at him as though she could not believe what he was saying. "Whatever do you mean, Lord Tomlin?"

"After the business of the painting, which I would rather forget, her father and I got together. He has no money, you see, he keeps on that great rambling old house and it costs him a fortune. Anyway, to cut a long story short, I offered to pay for Cressida's model training. It's the only thing she wants to do and I think she would make a good model. It's a tough business and I think that Cressy can be quite ruthless when she tries. I'm telling you all this, but very few people will know that I'm footing the bill. I can afford it and it will give me pleasure; Samuel was feeling very badly about the painting and he realizes that she needs to be away from home and doing what she has always wanted to do. So it didn't take much to persuade him." He stopped and looked at her and smiled. "It's a long story, Beth, what do you think of it?"

She smiled back. "I think you're nothing short of a wizard," she said, and they both laughed. "And you put me to shame, I'd really got it in for Cressida after the scene she created and I was not prepared to be in the least charitable. You are a dear, you really are. What does Alex think about it?" she asked him.

"He was very enthusiastic, he even took her up to London. She started the new term straight after Easter, we didn't lose any time and she had no trouble getting in; she's sharing a flat with another girl. The model school fixed that up for her, so her father isn't worried about her." He stopped to think for a moment, as though pondering some difficulty. "When Alex came back from London, he was so pleased, as though it was a relief to him. But since then, he has got more and more — well, sour-faced, I think it is the only word. He seems to be snapping at us all, even James."

Beth remembered that Laura had said something similar.

"Perhaps he is missing Cressida," she suggested.

Lord Tomlin got to his feet and looked at her. "I don't myself think that it is Cressida he is missing."

He said no more and started to walk towards the door. "I have kept you a long time, Beth, and I haven't even bought a painting." He looked out at the street where the sun was shining on the small shops and houses.

"It's a lovely day, what are you going

to do with yourself with your half-day? Not staying in, I hope."

She held the door open for him. "No, I am going over to Dunwich Cliff, it's my favourite place on a day like this and it's very quiet at this time of year."

"Good girl, have a good walk and don't forget what I've said to you. I mean every word. Goodbye, Beth."

Beth watched his tall, straight figure walk down the street; he and Alex are alike, she thought. I sometimes think that Alex has got his father's kindness too, I've had one or two glimpses of it. What a rogue his father is, she said to herself, and had a chuckle as she ate her lunch and got herself ready to go walking at Dunwich.

10

WHEN Beth reached the cliff car-park at Dunwich, she was reminded vividly of the last time she had been there and James had fallen into the sea. It was a happy day, she thought, there seemed to have been these little oases in the troubled time at Haversham.

As she walked along the broad beach path towards Sizewell, the wind was fresh from the south but not cold. The sun was shining in a sky peppered with white clouds that did not obscure it for very long; a perfect walking day, she said to herself.

The act of walking quickly always freed the mind from its power to dwell on problems, and helped to sort them out. And for Beth, this day was no exception. Uppermost and echoing through her were the things that Lord

Tomlin had said that morning. After the guilt of her bitter feelings towards Cressida, she felt pleased that the girl had at last got her heart's desire. She thought of Alex and wondered if he missed Cressida or whether it was a case of out of sight, out of mind.

She could not imagine him taciturn, as his father had described him and it gave her a longing to be with him to see if she had the power to bring the smile back into his eyes. But she reasoned that Lord Tomlin had been quite wrong when he had hinted that it was not Cressida that he was missing, but herself. Alex knew where she lived, he knew where the shop was, but in all the weeks since their quarrel, he had never once sought her out.

She had passed the hide and did not go in; the memories seemed hard to bear. She walked on, still trying to sort out past emotions, when she heard the sound of running footsteps behind her and in her imagination, thought she heard the sound of her name.

Without warning, and giving her an initial shock, her shoulders were grabbed from behind and she was forced to stop.

"Beth, Beth," came the gasping voice of Alex. "I thought you would never stop."

She did not have time to see the expression in his eyes. He had seized her and pulled her to him, wrapping his arms right round her as though he had found something he had been seeking for a long time. His breath still coming quickly, he laid his head on top of her hair.

Such was the surprise, that Beth did not move, but gave herself to the wonderful feeling of coming home to the place where she most wanted to be. She did not try to question, to seek reasons, she laid her head against his thumping heart and waited.

As he raised his head he whispered, "Beth, is it really you?"

She looked up and was given no chance to reply. His lips descended on hers and his kiss transported her into a world where there was only Alex, and an Alex she could be close to and also to love.

She was the first to speak and her voice too was a whisper. "What are you doing here, Alex?" she asked him.

"I came to find you," was all he said and he kissed her again, lightly and playfully as though all he wanted was the confirmation of touch and the knowledge that she really was in his arms.

"Don't say any more," he said. "Let's walk down to that breakwater and we can lean back and sit in the sun, and I can tell you why I am here."

They strolled with arms entwined like lovers, Beth was still content not to question but to enjoy this feeling of oneness with the man who had been so much in her thoughts and in her heart.

As they reached the old wooden breakwater, Alex took her in his arms once again before they sat down. His lips and his hands seemed to be telling her things that he had not voiced in words, and she was filled with a wild joy and hope.

"Beth," he said at last, "I have so wanted to see you, but I dared not come. There is something I want to ask you but I did not know what you would say. You were so angry with me, and yet I could have explained if you would have let me."

"Cressida would have taken a lot of explaining Alex." She still felt aggrieved in spite of the deep-down feeling that things were coming right. "Beth, I will ask you first, will you believe what I tell you, implicitly, without question?"

"Yes," she said in a small voice. "I don't think you would lie to me."

"I will try to explain to you, though it's a long story. To me there always has been Cressida, you've got to remember that there are ten years between us, so I knew her right from her being a baby. After her mother was killed in that road accident, Cressida was practically brought up in our house, so she has always been like a little sister to me. Do you understand what I'm saying, Beth? She's like a little sister."

"But . . . "

He stopped her. "No buts yet, you've got to let me finish. As she grew up, she followed me everywhere; not Stephen, he was that much older. Then when she was about fifteen, she fell for me in a big way, I was her idol. I was twenty-five then and had one or two broken romances behind me, and I suppose it amused me. I know now that I was wrong, but I didn't know at the time; I didn't take her seriously, neither did I realize how serious she was. When she swore she was going to marry me when she was older, I suppose I just kidded her along, thinking that she would grow out of her crush for me in a few months."

He took her hands and held them tight. "Beth, I didn't come here to talk about Cressida, I want to talk about you," he said.

"No, I want it all out in the open, there are still questions unanswered. Go on, Alex, I don't mind." Beth was firm and sure in her reply.

"Well, it turned out that Cressida did think I was serious; she didn't leave home, she didn't forget me, and she was beginning to embarrass me though I didn't want to hurt her. It all came to a head when you came along, she became more clinging and jealous at the same time, and I suppose I didn't know how to handle it. I know that sounds feeble but I truly didn't want the girl hurt and in any case, I thought she would be going off to model school at any moment, and once she was there she would soon forget all about me." He paused for a moment and Beth looked at his troubled face.

Then she spoke to him. "She told me that when you were married, you would buy her a flat in town while she was modelling and that she would come back to you at weekends." Beth wanted to see what Alex would make of this.

He whistled. "The little so-and-so," he exclaimed vehemently. "She was making it up to suit herself and to impress you at the same time. It wasn't true, you know, Beth."

Alex sounded very sincere and Beth believed him.

"I suppose I must feel sorry for her," she said. "But it has been very hard, especially after the affair of the painting, I didn't have very nice thoughts about her after that."

Her hands were taken to his lips and he held them there. "Beth, I think we've got to take the lead from Father; I did all I could to help Cressida after we came back from Edinburgh and then he stepped in."

Beth knew he was right and she liked the feel of his lips on her fingers; she was smiling up at him as she spoke.

"I believe you, Alex, but there is one thing I cannot forget and it was the cause of our quarrel. It seems to haunt me; after we came back from Cambridge, after that lovely day, you were all over her as though I didn't exist, and it was only because she was put out because you had taken me and not her. I was sure it was Cressida you loved and I have thought so ever since."

"Oh, Beth," he groaned. "I suppose I have some kindness left in me." And Beth remembered how she had compared him to his father. "I was sorry for Cressy, it was my little sister all over again; there was no more to it than that and I just couldn't understand why you were so angry. We'd had such a lovely day and suddenly it all went wrong."

He framed her face in his hands. "Beth, for months now, there has been only one person I wanted to love and she is looking into my eyes at the moment. I love you, Beth, will you believe me?"

He kissed her gently and she eagerly returned the soft pressure of his lips. Her dream had come true and he had said the words she had longed to hear.

He looked into her eyes again and saw the love shining there.

"My Beth, does it mean . . . are you going to tell me you love me?"

"I love you, Alex."

She was crushed in his arms and into the embrace and the kiss went all the feeling of those last few months; jealousy and quarrels were forgotten, there only remained the love that they had to show one another.

"Alex."

"Yes, love."

"I'm sorry, I'm still thinking of things; why didn't you come to the shop after Cressida had gone to London? I know you were miserable and I was longing to see you," she said.

"But, Beth, how was I to know that? You'd said you never wanted to see me again and I thought you hated me for how I'd behaved towards Cressida. There had been a time when I thought you were coming to love me, but that day everything fell in ruins. I thought you would soon forget me once you were back in the shop."

She smiled at him. "I missed you, Alex."

"Not as much as I missed you, I thought I was destined to be a bachelor until you came along."

"You are not going to remain a bachelor then, Alex?" Beth couldn't resist the teasing tone.

"It depends on the answer to my question," he said, kissing her again.

"What question?" she asked.

"I've got a good mind not to ask you, Beth Carrington, but I must, mustn't I? I can't wait any longer. Will you marry me, Beth? Please, Beth."

"I wouldn't like you to remain a bachelor, Alex."

"Beth?" His tone was threatening.

"Yes, please, I would like to marry you." She was quiet while he kissed her, but her mind kept raising questions.

"But, Alex. Oh dear, I keep thinking of obstacles. What about Cressida, does she still think you are going to marry her one day?"

"She does not," he exploded. "I let her know where she stood before I left her in London. I told her in no uncertain terms that I was going to marry you, and it was time she grew up and forgot me . . . "

"Alex, you can't have done," was Beth's startled reply. "You hadn't asked me."

"I know," he said, and gave her a kiss. "But I felt so sure, and do you know when I felt certain of you, Beth?"

She shook her head.

"Sitting in the chapel at King's College; you felt the same, didn't you?"

She smiled. "Yes, I did, it was when I was sure that what I felt for you was love. Oh, Alex, we've been so foolish, but I suppose it doesn't matter now that we've found each other."

For a long time they stayed locked in each other's arms with no heed for the fresh wind that came with the incoming tide. Beth felt as though her heart was bursting with happiness, so sure was she in her love for Alex and his for her.

It was Alex who broke the silence. "I think we'd better go home and tell the family, don't you? I'll race you to the cars."

She took up the challenge with a laugh and they arrived at the cars panting and out of breath. His arm came around her as they looked back along the stretch of open beach, with the sea thundering white against the pebbles of the shore.

"This will always be our special place," he said, with his lips against her hair.

"Alex," Beth suddenly thought of something. "Alex, how on earth did you find me here?"

He roared with laughter. "It was my wicked papa; he came over to the farm after lunch and said that he didn't wish to interfere in my affairs, but there was a certain girl who was looking very sad and who was going walking at Dunwich

Cliff on her afternoon off when she had shut her shop."

"He's a rogue," said Beth, but she couldn't stop laughing. "He spent nearly the whole morning with me and had told me about Cressida going to London and that you were miserable. I didn't know what to think; we will have to go and tell him, won't we?"

It didn't take them long to get back to Haversham Hall, where they sought both Lord Tomlin and Laura, who received their news with much joy. Beth joined Alex to walk over to the farm, feeling that she had stepped into a ready-made family.

They had a meal together and before the sun disappeared, they strolled across the fields in an aura of contentment. Alex stopped walking at the point where a group of elms at the top of a field looked over the whole of the farm and Haversham Hall. He pulled her to him and she couldn't have got free if she had wanted to try.

"You're a wonderful, wonderful girl,"

he said as he looked about him. "This is going to be our home, Beth, our land and our home. Do you like it? Will you be happy here?"

"I love it," she told him, then her arms wound round his neck and she touched his lips with hers. "And I love you most of all."

He kissed her for a long time, and at last they made their way back to the farm, sure in the knowledge that this was what each of them wanted and that they had a world of togetherness and love in front of them.

THE END

Other titles in the Linford Romance Library:

A YOUNG MAN'S FANCY
Nancy Bell

Six people get together for reasons of their own, and the result is one of misunderstanding, suspicion and mounting tension.

THE WISDOM OF LOVE
Janey Blair

Barbie meets Louis and receives flattering proposals, but her reawakened affection for Jonah develops into an overwhelming passion.

MIRAGE IN THE MOONLIGHT
Mandy Brown

En route to an island to be secretary to a multi-millionaire, Heather's stubborn loyalty to her former flatmate plunges her into a grim hazard.

WITH SOMEBODY ELSE
Theresa Charles

Rosamond sets off for Cornwall with Hugo to meet his family, blissfully unaware of the shocks in store for her.

A SUMMER FOR STRANGERS
Claire Hamilton

Because she had lost her job, her flat and she had no money, Tabitha agreed to pose as Adam's future wife although she believed the scheme to be deceitful and cruel.

VILLA OF SINGING WATER
Angela Petron

The disquieting incidents that occurred at the Vatican and the Colosseum did not trouble Jan at first, but then they became increasingly unpleasant and alarming.

DOCTOR NAPIER'S NURSE
Pauline Ash

When cousins Midge and Derry are entered as probationer nurses on the same day but at different hospitals they agree to exchange identities.

A GIRL LIKE JULIE
Louise Ellis

Caroline absolutely adored Hugh Barrington, but then Julie Crane came into their lives. Julie was the kind of girl who attracts men without even trying.

COUNTRY DOCTOR
Paula Lindsay

When Evan Richmond bought a practice in a remote country village he did not realise that a casual encounter would lead to the loss of his heart.